DC SUMNER

Merchant of Darkness

Contents

Acknowledgement   v

To The Reader   vi

The Mission   1

Research   7

A Turn For The Worst   12

How To Find A Lost City   20

Captives   26

Trials of Atlantis   33

Stone of Ruin   46

To The Lab   51

Enter Delirium   58

The Atlanteum   63

The Girl With The Atlantean Tattoo   71

Traitor   80

Kane Loses a Fight?   84

A Fast Trip Home   89

Prison Break   96

A Close Call   101

Lost and Found   112

The Vision   120

Sunset Crest   131

Youthful Advice   143

Joining The Fight   151

When a Bad Idea Sounds Good   156

The Might of an Atlantean 165
Corruptor of Souls 172
Subconscious Sanctum 188
Epilogue 198
About the Author 202
Also by DC Sumner 203

Acknowledgement

First and foremost, I thank my Lord and Savior, Jesus Christ for giving me all that I have.

To my family, who stood by me through the highs and lows of the creative process – your love and understanding have been my anchor.

My heartfelt thanks to my friends who lent their ears, provided valuable feedback, and cheered me on during moments of doubt.

To the writing community, both online and offline, thank you for sharing your wisdom, experiences, and camaraderie. Your collective spirit fueled my passion for storytelling.

Finally, to the readers who embark on this adventure with me, your curiosity and open hearts give purpose to the words on these pages. Thank you for joining me in this world of imagination.

I wish you all the best in your endeavors.

—DC Sumner

To The Reader

Dear reader, thank you for you continued support. This endeavor would not be possible without all of you. Don't forget to leave a review on Amazon/GoodReads! Reviews help indie authors to get more traffic on their works, so by leaving a review you are helping me get my stories out to the world!

The Mission

The yellow moon peaked out from behind a sliver of gray clouds. Ash crept around as quietly as possible with his squad mates scattered around in the jungle around him. They entered the training field where the enemy's home base had been set up. He gripped his bow tight, retrieving one of the blunt-tipped arrows from his quiver. He looked over at his squad leader, Adonis, who was giving the signal to begin their attack.

Training exercises had become more and more frequent as they waited with fearful anticipation for the next disaster to strike. So far, there had been no more attacks since Aros took over Ash's body, Killed Ember, and poisoned the Great Tree. No plans had been made as to how they were going to the heal the Tree and Ash dared not think of Ember. That wound was still too fresh to inspect. No, he was perfectly content with the battle simulations for the time being.

Ash readied his arrow and aimed at the guard closest to him. He imbued the blunt arrow with lightning magic and loosed it. The arrow zipped through the air with so much speed that it would have been impossible to see if not for the amethyst crackling around it. It struck its target in the chest, sending the man falling to the ground and clutching his chest. He'd be okay.

"Move in!" Adonis shouted and the squad converged around the walls of the structure.

The flag they were trying to retrieve was at the top of the fortress, waving in the breeze. They had been ordered to retrieve the flag by any means necessary, without harming comrades of course. Ash watched as the wind mages began lifting themselves up the walls of the base. He had become concerned with the lack of response from the opposing team. It was a simple 'capture the flag' exercise; Kane led the opposite squad, ordered to protect the flag.

Just as one of the wind mages was about to reach the flag, the walls of the structure exploded, sending all of Ash's squad sprawling to safety. He was flattened by a wall as the enemy team stormed out, trampling over the downed slats of wood. From where he lay, Ash could see the flashing of flames as the mages began to battle over control of the flag.

Ash tried to push himself up but the weight of the wall was too much. He was becoming increasingly frustrated. Luckily, the last person stepped off the platform and he was able to escape. After recovering to his feet, he noticed that there were roughly five enemies in front of him. He summoned the energy from his gut and let it flow out, bolts of purple lightning flared from his fingertips and struck each of the opponents in front of him. It wasn't enough to *really* harm them, but they dropped to the ground anyway as per the rules of the training exercise.

People were dropping all around him and, upon turning around, Ash realized that the flag seemed to be unguarded. Many of the outer walls were missing from their fortress and a spiral staircase stood in the center of the building that led straight up to the roof where the flag was. It was his for the taking.

Ash bolted for the stairs. A water mage leaped out from a hiding spot, swinging his fist at Ash who narrowly dodged it. Ash tried to strike him with his bow, but the mage blocked it with a burst of water. Ash re-attacked quickly by shooting a blast of lightning at the man's sternum. He clutched his smoldering shirt and dropped down with a scowl on his face.

Ash ran past him and began climbing the stairs. Reaching the opening to the roof, he didn't want to waste any time. He immediately reached for the flag. He was mere inches from claiming victory for his squad when a tendril of water whipped itself around his wrist and yanked him off the platform. He was plummeting towards the Earth.

Bracing for impact, Ash closed his eyes and grimaced, but the impact never came. He opened his eyes to see Quinn and Kane, smirks on their faces. Kane held a palm out toward him, using his control of the winds to keep the boy afloat. Ash made a sour face as Kane set him on the ground gently.

"Come on, man. I was so close," Ash complained to his friends.

Kane retorted, "You only got so close because that's what we wanted to happen."

"Now, boys. No need to get your underwear in a bunch," Quinn chuckled, "It's all fun and games."

Ash was still annoyed, "Yeah, you're right. I'll beat you one day, Kane."

"Maybe, but not today." The white-haired boy winked at Ash.

"Everyone stop!" Avani's voice echoed throughout the field. "Alpha squad has successfully defeated everyone in Bravo. The exercise is now over. Let's regroup at the Guild building and debrief. After that, we can all get some rest."

When Ash had first met him, Avani seemed to be one of those guys who was mad at everything and everyone. Now, he had really stepped into his role of being a Guardian. A leader amongst the other mages. Ash no longer was afraid to go to Avani with questions or to ask for advice from him.

Several months had gone by since the Great Tree was attacked. With each day that passed, the Tree became sicker. The black veins continued to spread through its bark and the leaves were falling. She had been silent since her last message. Ash still vividly remembered the vision he'd been granted by the Tree. Gethin, she called herself. He knew that he would have to be one of the three mages sent on the quest to save her, but no news had come down from the Guardians.

When Ash went to Avani or the others he was usually brushed off with, "Oh, we're still working on a plan" or something to that effect. What could he do? He wasn't in charge and didn't know where to start. All he could do was wait for orders. In the meantime, Kane, Quinn, and himself trained together rather consistently. Ash had gotten better at controlling his powers and had also become more efficient with other weapons. The bow and arrow was still his strong suit, but he wasn't too shabby with a sword now.

There was a guild meeting every two weeks so that the Guardians could discuss anything they deemed important enough to talk about. So far, there had been no updates as to the whereabouts of the Forbidden. All of their members and resources in the pit had seemingly vanished without a trace. Ash wondered why they hadn't attacked the Tree sooner if they were so close and when he brought it up to the Guardians, they told him it was most likely just so they could get their hands on him first.

Ash also wondered why the Great Tree didn't know where the Forbidden was. He made a mental note to ask her the next time she granted him a vision. He'd visited the Tree many times since the last vision and hadn't received so much as a peep, nor had anyone else to his knowledge. His best assumption was that she was conserving energy.

The Guild building was bustling with mages. Once all the Guardians took the stage the noise died down. Ember stayed standing while the other three took a seat. Ash noticed they'd been deferring to let him speak more often lately. It was strange. He was the newest of the Guardians, and yet, he seemed to be running the show half the time.

"My fellow Guild members, a quick congratulations goes to team Alpha on their victory tonight." Applause and congratulatory shouts echoed around the auditorium. "The other Guardians and I are very proud of all the hard work you all have done for these past few months. It does not go unnoticed. We know you all are anxious to know what we plan to do about the Great Tree. We have had much deliberation over this as of late, and the next step we believe to be vital is to gather research. We will need your help. Pour through any book or text of our world and report back to us with anything of substance that you may find. We believe the answer lies within our records."

"What should we look for?" Someone in the crowd shouted.

Ember seemed annoyed, "Look for anything related to relics that could save the Great Tree, obviously." He cleared his throat, "Now then. Be sure to alert us of anything of value that you find. This is your mission for now."

Ash hadn't done much reading as of late and was excited at the notion of being able to relax for a bit. So much of his time had been consumed by training that he was unable to hang out with his friends outside of sparring, grappling, weapons drilling, or field exercises. They were almost always around each other, but it felt like they were beginning to drift apart. The following day he would get to spend some quality time with them, however, at the time being, all he wanted to do was go to sleep.

Research

Ash and Quinn's relationship—if it could be called that—hadn't blossomed into anything more than an awkward exchange of showing slight affection to one another. Ash couldn't bring himself to muster the courage to ask her out on a proper date. Even if he did, he wasn't exactly original enough to just come up with something for them to do. This wasn't New York where they could go catch a movie or eat at a fancy restaurant. They didn't even have anything remotely similar in Asmaria.

Still, their friendship remained as strong as ever and the two would occasionally find themselves on the precipice of being together. They didn't celebrate holidays or birthdays in the same way Ash was used to but had their own way of honoring traditions. On birthdays, the person who was being celebrated would do something nice for their parents, seeing as they are the ones who brought them into the world. Ash thought it was beautiful in a humble sort of way.

Even with that knowledge, Ash wanted to do something special for her. He searched the beaches around the island, looking for the perfect stone to make his idea come to life. After several days, he came upon a teal rock in the shallow waters. With the help of Rick, Ash was able to shape the stone into a smooth oval and set it into a necklace. After he gave it to her, the way her eyes lit up left him ecstatic. She never took the thing off and he was almost certain that something would happen between them, but it didn't.

Much to Ash's surprise, Quinn had apparently been doing some research on American holidays. The time for Valentine's Day rolled around and she gifted him with a small brown bracelet with a purple lightning bolt charm on it. He adored it especially. He vowed to keep it with him at all times.

Asmaria was Ash's home for many months, but he still felt different, and out of place. He knew he was different of course. He was a singular lightning wielder amongst a sea of elemental mages. The only person close to being as strange as he was was Rick, and he didn't understand what it was like to have this power thrust upon him. Ever since meeting his biological father, Ash started calling Rick by his name. He didn't mean for it to be disrespectful or anything, and Rick assured him that he didn't mind; he just felt weird calling him dad after knowing his birth father was alive. Ash could've let being an outcast bother him, but he chose to lean into the singularity with his outward appearance.

Ash put together his daily ensemble by cutting away some of the material from his purple tunic and then was able to get his hands on a pair of dark brown shorts. Of course, he still wore his Converse; those just felt like... *him.* Naturally, his looks garnered the looks of passersby when he'd walk down the street, but he got used to it, and, eventually, so did they.

Ash, Quinn, and Kane were going through the tomes in the Asmarian library as quickly as possible. The bookkeepers were probably annoyed by all the noise they were making, considering they'd shushed the group of kids several times. Ash saw several other mages filtering in and out throughout the day.

After hours of mind-numbing research, they still hadn't found anything they would consider important. Ash began to think back to what Gethin had said. Her riddle involved a kingdom that was lost at sea. He'd start there. Ash remembered learning about a mythical kingdom called Atlantis. Something about Atlantis was closely related to the sea but he couldn't remember it exactly.

Turning to his friends, "Have you guys ever heard of Atlantis?"

"The lost city? Yeah," Kane said.

Quinn said, "I can't believe no one has thought of that yet. You're a genius!"

Ash was beaming. "I remember hearing about it, but I can't quite remember many of the details. Beside it being lost under the sea or something."

Kane chimed in, "Brilliant. Let's start looking for anything related to Atlantis."

They scoured the library, searching high and low until finally, Quinn found it. A heavy book titled, 'Mythical Lands From A-Z'. She brought it back over to their shared table and laid down, blowing dust off the cover. She slowly cracked it open, and they began rifling through its brown pages. Luckily what they were looking for began with the letter A.

"Here it is!" Quinn said, "Atlantis—the city swallowed by the sea. There's even drawn pictures of what it supposedly looked like."

Ash took in every detail he could. He found it to be a rather beautiful and intriguing place. The painted picture was an aerial view of the kingdom. It was very circular. He noticed that it appeared to be built into sandbars surrounded by water. It gave the appearance that the kingdom was floating in the ocean. There was an outer ring with a gap which was most likely used for boats to enter and exit. Along the outer ring were buildings placed among a multitude of trees. Boats were harbored around the outer edges of the ring.

On the inside of the outer ring was water and beyond that another circle that appeared to be one solid building all the way around. More trees and water lay in between that one and the very center. In the center was a tall palace made of shimmering gold.

After taking in the drawings of the city, he began reading the content of the legend that was Atlantis. There were many different theories as to what happened to the city. Some believe that it was swallowed by a massive flood. Others believe that it was ravaged by earthquakes and thus sank to the bottom of the sea. And then some believe the kingdom never existed at all and is simply the figment of a crazed man's imagination.

"This has to be it." Ash said, "We've not found anything else. No one has. This has got to be the right answer. If only Gethin could just tell us."

"Oh, come on. The mystery is what makes it fun!" Kane said.

Ash read aloud, "From the journal of King Atlan whom Atlantis is named after: *Many have tried to take us. All have failed. Atlantis stands strong but I fear our reign will soon end. My boy searches for that which will save us all. I pray to the Gods that he returns with good news soon. If our demise rings true, take to the sky, and look for the eye. There, shall we be.*"

Kane huffed, "Great. More riddles."

"You're not much of a thinker, are you?" Ash asked playfully which resulted in a punch to the arm from Kane.

Quinn said, "We have to get this to the Guardians. They'll know what to do."

A Turn For The Worst

The Guardian's offices were in the Guild building. Each office resembled the leader's respective element. The three kids walked down the hall to their offices with the large heavy book in hand. Ember's office door was the only one open.

Ash had an uneasy feeling as they approached the orange room. The new Guardian always made Ash feel awkward when the two of them were together. He hadn't been alone with the man yet and wanted to keep it that way. He could see sconces with orange flames dancing along the walls of the room. Ember was sitting at his desk, staring down at a flurry of papers. It would seem the Guardian's job didn't only consist of protecting Asmaria.

Quinn knocked on the door and stepped across the threshold, "Excuse me, sir."

He held up his hand without looking up, gesturing for them to wait. And then he looked up with an annoyed expression, "What is it?"

"We found something we think may be important."

"You *think?*"

Quinn hesitated, "Well… We're pretty sure."

He didn't respond, just held out his hand. Quinn walked over and opened to the section that talked about Atlantis. He read the few pages in silence once and then again. When he finished, he closed the book and said, "I see nothing of significance here. Don't waste my time again."

Ash stepped forward, "But sir—"

"I said I see nothing of significance here. Now leave." Ash was completely thrown off by the brashness of the Guardian. How could he not see that this was the answer? Fine, if he didn't want to listen then they would just have to go to the others. He moved forward to grab the book.

Ember yanked the book off his desk and threw it into a drawer in his desk, slamming it shut. "You will mention this to no one."

None of them said anything. They simply turned and walked out of his office.

Kane finally spoke, "We are definitely getting that book back. I have a bad feeling about that guy."

Ash said, "He's given me the creeps from day one."

With the cover of nightfall, Ash and his friends sneaked through the Guild building. They found Ember's office door shut and locked. Of course, it wouldn't be that easy for them. However, they were determined to get the book back and warn the other Guardians. Ash just hoped the book was still in his desk.

"How do we get in if the door is locked?" Ash asked.

"I think I've got us covered." Quinn closed her eyes and placed a hand on the doorknob. The other was an inch away and began conjuring a small amount of fluid that inserted itself into the keyhole. She stayed focused on the task at hand for several moments and then they heard a distinct click. She turned the knob and the door swung inward. They rushed in and Kane retrieved the book from Ember's desk.

The following morning, they found the other Guardians out on the training field. Taking turns so as not to leave out any details and told them everything. From the moment they found the book containing information on Atlantis and their theory that this was where they should go to look for a cure. And then how they'd come the prior day to show them, but Ember told them it was a waste of time.

By the end of their rendition of this tale, Avani seemed to be fuming. "I knew we shouldn't have chosen him. He's always been unpredictable!"

"Who are we to argue with who the people choose? We'd be no better than dictators if we overruled them." Bora made a good point.

Leena said, "Let's just go talk to him. Perhaps he had a good reason for doing what he did."

"I do have a reason for doing what I did." No one saw Ember come up from behind their group. "It seems we have a little mutiny on our hands." Ash could see the hint of a smile on Ember's face.

Leena tried to diffuse the situation, "Ember, that's not what's happening at all. We just want to know the truth of what happened."

"I'll tell you what happened. I used my judgment to keep our people from going on a wild goose chase. Or better yet, led into a trap by *him*." He pointed at Ash.

"What do you mean?" Avani asked.

"You all think it was a coincidence that the boy was used to destroy the Great Tree? He's evil! He's working with the enemy and you're all too blind to see it! He'll lead us all to our deaths and help Aros plunge the world into darkness!"

Ash couldn't believe what he was hearing, but before he could interject, Ember became crazier. "And you know what I think? I think his two little friends are his accomplices. There's no way that he could infiltrate our home so effortlessly without help! I say we lock them all up!"

Say what you want about him, but Ash wouldn't stand idly by while someone so openly insults his friends. "How dare y—." The ground beneath him rumbled and in a flash, he and his friends were swallowed up to their necks by dirt. "What the heck!" He yelled.

"If you're so sure," Avani said, "we'll put it up for a vote. See what the Guild thinks. If they agree then we can lock them up for good."

Bora said, "Avani, what are you doing?"

"Ember is a fellow Guardian. If he's so sure about this then we need to give him the benefit of the doubt. Maybe we have gotten too close to these three."

Ash turned as much as he could to look at his friends. Their mouths were slackly open with the same amount of shock that he felt. "How could you do this?" he shouted. He sank even further into the ground, dirt covering his mouth.

"Not another word." Avani's gaze bore into Ash's soul.

The Asmarian prison was especially depressing for Ash. He remembered always feeling like a prisoner when he was living in the apartment with Rick. Rick—who loved him as his own son—never realized how Ash felt until it was too late. Looking back, Ash felt dumb for feeling like his home was a prison. It was nothing like this. They had been taken underground, their hands bound to keep them from being able to wield any magic.

There were four walls made completely of stone. It was dark

and cold. There was no light whatsoever and that truly made Ash feel like he was going insane. He had no way to keep track of time apart from when meals were brought to him. He tried counting the seconds between meals but gave up after reaching 1,000. He didn't know if Kane and Quinn were close to him or not. He couldn't hear anything except the stone grinding to open a slot for food to be inserted. There was a little light that would shine through, just enough for him to grab the food before the slot closed again.

After talking to himself for what felt like the millionth time, the stone began to grind open again. This time, however, it wasn't just a food slot opening. It was a hole large enough to walk through. The light that poured through was nearly blinding. He scooted into a corner, curled up with his knees to his chest, covering his eyes with his forearm at an awkward angle.

"Ash. Get up." The voice said. He recognized it but was delirious. "Come on. It's time for your judgment." And then hands were on him, hurling him to his feet. He peeked through his eyes, trying to adjust to the light. He shuffled along with a hand clamped to his arm. Eventually, he was able to open his eyes completely and saw that it was Avani leading him to the Guild building.

"What's going on?" Ash's voice sounded rough. He hadn't used it in—there was no telling—how long. He looked around and didn't see anyone else.

"Do you have your faculties about you? What I'm about to say can't be forgotten. The events that follow today will be crucial. Do you understand?"

"I guess so." Ash wasn't sure what Avani was talking about still.

"Right now, Kane and Quinn are waiting for us at the Guild building. They've already been filled in on what I'm going to tell you. Ember is going to make the case that you all are traitors. If the Guild disagrees then you will be set free and we will figure out how to convince everyone to send you to Atlantis. If things go the opposite way and the Guild agrees then Leena, Bora, and I will be forced to lock you back up.

"However, I am the Guardian of earth and luckily, that's what our prison is made of. I will find a way to set you free and the three of you will need to immediately leave for Atlantis. It will be up to you to find the key to saving the Great Tree. Do you understand everything I've told you?"

Ash nodded, "I understand. One thing I don't get is why this is happening. Ember is supposed to be a Guardian. How could someone so insane take that position?"

"Well, every group of people is going to have a few eccentrics. Ember just so happens to be well-liked amongst many of the Guild members. He's also a very powerful fire mage. It makes sense if you think about it."

Kane could hear murmurs throughout the crowd. He was still in utter shock that he found himself in this position. He was a prodigy among his peers and yet, he was on trial for treason. He wasn't as optimistic as other people. Kane assumed that Quinn was thinking the Guild would be on their side just because innocence is on their side. However, he vividly remembers the way they acted when Ember was first elected as a Guardian. The mob was so prepared to attack Ash.

He blocked out Ember's voice as the man pled the case that all three of them were traitors and deserving of punishment. Kane didn't care to hear it all over again. It was the same speech he'd given to the other Guardians, more or less. He was riling them up, that's for sure. By the time he stopped talking the majority of the crowd was on their feet, shouting and pumping their fists in the air.

"If you vote in favor of the kids, please stand," Leena said to the crowd.

Not to Kane's surprise, most of them remained seated. "And now if you vote to imprison them, please stand." The verdict was clear. Much of the Guild, many of whom Kane had trained with over the years, had voted to send them to prison. They would be there for life, as was customary for traitors. Or so they thought.

Kane was excited. It almost seemed easier this way. Had they been found innocent, there would have been more work in figuring out who to send to search for Atlantis. Now, they would just need to wait to be rescued by the other Guardians from their holds and then they'd be on their way.

Kane was back in the cold, dark dungeon. He was patiently waiting for the stone to slide open and make his escape. It finally came after what he assumed had been several hours. The wall in front of him ground open, revealing the three Guardians who weren't insane. Quinn and Ash were with them, already freed from imprisonment. The Guardians handed the gear bags to each of them. Ash already had his bow and quiver slung across his back. Avani freed Kane's hands and he flexed his fingers, working the cold out of them.

Avani's eyes were wide, "We must hurry. Ember wanted to come visit you all. He'll be here any minute now."

They sprinted up the stone steps that led to the surface of the earth. Bora shot a blast of wind at it, flinging it open. As they rushed out of the ground, Ember stood a few paces away, staring at them. "What are you doing?" he seethed.

Avani stepped in front of them, "What you've done isn't right. We're here to fix it."

Ember's hands erupted in flames and his eyes glowed bright orange. The others got into battle stances. Leena turned to the kids, "Go! Run!"

Kane was the first to move. He was the most experienced of the three and knew they would look to him for guidance. Flames passed over his shoulder as they ran. He glanced back and saw Ember hurling fireballs at them but was then subdued by the other Guardians. He didn't know what would happen to them, but it wasn't something he could worry about right now. Their mission was more important than any other in all of Asmaria's history. Never had the Tree been in such grave danger.

Now was the problem of how they were going to find Atlantis. As if reading his mind, he saw Quinn pull a small object from her pocket. The Guardians must have given the horn to her. It was common knowledge that only they were allowed to have such an item. She blew the horn, emitting the tiniest of sounds. A sound so high-pitched that it was hardly audible to their ears.

They kept running and within a couple minutes, Kane heard the sound of wings beating in the air. He looked up and saw the mighty dragons circling over them. The massive beasts dove toward them and landed a few meters away. They ran up to the dragons and climbed upon their backs. Kane asked Vesta, the great orange dragon, to head West and she launched into the air. The others followed closely. As they ascended with great speed, Kane looked to the ground and saw many of the Guild running around, elements flying. It looked like a civil war.

How To Find A Lost City

Quinn's hair whipped around her face as the wind passed by. She was fine for a while but soon enough, Kolora's scales began to make her thighs sore. She tried shifting around on the beast's back but there wasn't much room to move, and she did not want to fall from this height. They were flying over the ocean with islands popping up here and there, although from this altitude they were like ants to her eyes.

The dragons began to slow, their wings weary from the constant flying. Kolora followed Vesta as she descended through a fluffy cloud. There was a small island down below but it was big enough to hold some creatures of its own. She hoped there was some fresh water for them to drink as well; the moleskins in their packs weren't enough and she figured the amount the dragons needed would leave her dead if she tried conjuring that much.

They landed on the beach with a gentleness that surprised her coming from the large beasts. "Where do you think we are?" She asked, walking up to the boys as they stretched their weary limbs.

Kane said, "Fairly close to the Bermuda Triangle. That's

where we're headed. One of the theories of Atlantis' location is the Bermuda Triangle."

"Sounds like a plan to me," Ash said with a yawn.

The three of them walked along the beach making small talk while the dragons tramped around the island in search of a light snack. By the time they returned, the sun was already dropping in the sky, casting streaks of pink and orange across the horizon.

Kane said, "We'd better make camp here for the night. It's probably best not to venture into the Bermuda Triangle in the dark, considering the mysterious disappearances it's known for. It's famous even in Asmaria."

They assembled a large mound of logs and asked for the assistance of the dragons to start a fire. Iguru opened his mouth, a hiss issuing from his throat and a small flame curled out. The pile of wood ignited immediately. The dragon looked proud of himself.

Quinn was still worried about the other Asmarians they'd left behind. She too had seen them fighting as they left their home. She hoped there wouldn't be any casualties but knew that was probably just wishful thinking.

"I can't believe this is happening," she said. "Brandr would have never done something like this. Ember should never have taken his place." Quinn was fighting to hold back her tears as she thought about the passing of the Guardian.

"That's just it though," Ash said. "Ember can never really take his place. Not in here." He pointed to her heart and that was enough to make the well of tears slip down her cheeks.

She nodded her head but couldn't choke down the knot that was in her throat. Quinn was exhausted from the day of travel. She resorted to trying to get some sleep. She laid next to Ash, not touching him, but close enough to do so if she felt like it.

Ash felt something tickling his face. He thought it would go away but it persisted. He awoke slowly and was startled to find a small crab dancing on his cheek. Swatting it away, he sat up and looked around. The others were already up and about, packing up their gear bags. The dragons waited patiently on the shoreline.

"You guys couldn't wake me?" He asked.

Kane chuckled, "We thought you could use the beauty sleep."

"Oh, you have jokes, huh? Come on then." Ash put up his fists.

"Stop it, boys. The dragons will think there's something wrong with you." Quinn laughed.

Kane smiled slyly at her, "But there is something wrong with us."

"Just come on," she said.

Ash gathered up his gear and climbed back aboard the back of Iguru, patting the creature on his back. "Ready, buddy?" He asked him, to which he answered with a hum like a cat's purr.

With that, they launched into the air and filed in next to Kane and Vesta. Ash saw Kane turn around on Vesta's back, a small map unfolded in his hands. He didn't understand how Kane could know where they were with nothing but ocean, ocean, and more ocean around them.

Iguru floated in closer to Vesta and Ash saw Kolora do the same on the opposite side. Kane shouted over the roar of the wind, "If I'm correct, we're right above the Bermuda Triangle. We're going to drop down and get closer to the water."

Ash held up a thumb as all three dragons descended, pulling back to slow their speed as the water rushed up toward them. He had an off feeling about the waters below them and wanted to get out of there as quickly as possible. "Iguru, can you get me closer to Kane?" he asked the dragon who promptly tilted his body, gliding in next to Vesta. Kane looked over and Ash yelled, "I have a bad feeling about this place, I think we should get out of here!"

Before Kane had time to respond, a tentacle longer and thicker than Ash could have ever imagined ripped through the surface of the water. Vesta and Iguru were able to dodge it, but Kolora wasn't so lucky. It clipped her tail and sent her spiraling. Ash's stomach dropped as he watched Quinn fall from the dragon's back. Kolora recovered, leveling out just before touching the water. He saw Quinn resurface, seemingly uninjured, but then nothing happened when she tried to manipulate the water around her.

"Dive down!" he yelled to Iguru who responded accordingly.

The dragon flapped his massive wings, hovering just a few feet above Quinn. "What's the matter?" he yelled to her.

"My water magic isn't working!"

Ash was trying to think of what to do, although, critical thinking had never been his strong suit. Before he could come up with something, the water around her began to swirl. From this height and angle, Ash could see a large mouth taking shape beneath Quinn. He crouched on the dragon's back, aiming his palm at the creature.

"No!" Kane's shout interrupted him from zapping the beast below them. "You'll hit Quinn!"

Why hadn't he thought of that? Ash cursed himself for being so stupid. He would never forgive himself if he hurt her. He was thankful to have Kane there to keep him from being so reckless.

Ash saw Kane jump off Vesta's back, weaving hand signs to

control the wind, and yet nothing happened for him either. Luckily, Vesta noticed and caught him with her talons, dangling him upside down as they passed by Quinn. He reached down and grabbed her by the wrist, yanking her out of harm's way. They shot up into the sky as the beast below them ruptured the water, issuing an ear-splitting scream, clearly frustrated that its meal escaped.

This, Ash thought, *is what nightmares are made of.* The thing had so many tentacles they were uncountable. Its mouth was a large black beak and showed gnarly teeth that were bigger than Ash. It had eyes that were black as night. The mysterious disappearances related to this area were no longer that mysterious.

The dragons flew away in a haste and Ash saw Quinn hop from Vesta onto Kolora's back. He was thankful none of them were hurt, including the dragons. Ash noticed that he was gripping one of Iguru's spikes so tightly that his knuckles were turning white. They continued flying on, heading toward the next spot on Kane's map.

With all this time to think about things, Ash found himself worrying about Rick. He had left his adoptive father behind in Asmaria with not so much as a goodbye. Granted, he couldn't exactly take a detour from their prison escape to swing by and check out with the man. Still, though, he hoped nothing bad was happening to him. His best hope was that the other Guardians beat Ember in whatever battle occurred during their departure. If they were in charge, then he was confident Rick would be okay. But if they weren't, he didn't have much confidence that Rick would be left alone.

The next place on their map of possible Atlantis locations was in the Sahara Desert. They landed once more near a small forest so the dragons could replenish their energy and Ash took that time to voice his concerns.

"So, the kingdom of water is going to be in… the desert?" he asked Kane.

"I know, I know. It sounds ridiculous. But we have to exhaust all avenues that may lead us to the right place. This was just the next closest one."

"Okay, sounds crazy to me, but you're the boss."

"Please," Quinn said, "don't call him that. His head is already too big for his shoulders." She gave him a playful shove. Ash felt a twinge of jealousy come over him, but he shoved it down.

It was a good thing they stopped for a bit because this desert was much larger than Ash could have thought. He'd read about it before, but the sheer magnitude of the dunes of sand that stretched out for miles was overwhelming. It seemed like they'd flown for days before anything interesting happened.

Kane was gesturing for them to look down; miles below them, the ground had formed massive circles. It looked extremely similar to the picture of Atlantis they'd seen. The water, trees, and buildings were missing, but apart from that the shape was identical.

The area wasn't completely sand either; the circles had rocks jutting out all over the place. The dragons began their descent toward the rings, and they would soon find out if this was Atlantis or not. Ash had a good feeling that this was what they were looking for. But that feeling left quickly as he realized there were no buildings, people, or any sort of structure in this place. How were they going to find what they were looking for?

Captives

Avani, Leena, and Bora sat in the Guild building with their hands bound so tightly they wouldn't be able to do magic. Avani tried twisting around in the rope that held him to the wooden chair. It would seem that Ember had the overwhelming support of the younger mages in the Guild and overpowered them. Those who fought alongside them were given the choice to fall in line with Ember's ideals or be subject to the same imprisonment as the other Guardians. Not a single one of them chose to stand by their sides. If there were any on their side, they hadn't shown it during the altercation.

"I can't believe this has happened," Bora said.

"I should have never put it up to a vote. I should have killed him before he got the chance." Avani was seething pure hatred for the man at this point. That darkness creeping back up inside him.

Leena retorted, "Don't speak like that, Avani. None of us could have known that it was going to lead to this. I thought for sure we would have more support as well."

"What do we do now?" Bora asked.

Leena answered, "There's not much we can do other than try coming up with a plan of escape or wait this thing out.

"I know one thing's for sure," Avani said, "I won't miss another opportunity to end that fool of a Guardian."

As if on cue, the doors to the room they were being held in flew open, smacking the wall with a loud clang. Ember waltzed in, swinging his arms with a cocky swagger. Avani's nose crunched and his brows furrowed at the sight of him. Avani didn't think he'd ever wanted to hurt a fellow Asmarian so much before.

"Why the long faces, guys? Your little treacherous plan didn't come to fruition?"

"*Our* plan?" Avani began. "You're the one who—"

"Avani, don't," Leena said. "Don't give him anything."

"Oh, come on. Don't be like that. I was bound to take over sooner or later. Whether I used the kid to do it or not doesn't matter. I was always going to push you three aside and gain control of the Guild."

Avani was thrown off a bit. He was going to do this regardless, so he just used Ash to turn the Guild into an angry, vicious mob. This didn't help Avani's mood in the slightest.

"But why?" Bora asked. "What's the point in all this?"

"It's simple really," Ember said, matter-of-factly. "The other humans in this world are weak. And their weakness is killing the Earth. I know it's generally not accepted to travel to other parts of the world, however, I've left Asmaria several times. In my travels, I've learned things about humans from different lands that would make your skin crawl. The acts of murder and death they spread with such ease is abhorrent, to say the least."

"So, you mean to what, kill them all?" Avani asked, generally curious at this point.

Ember laughed, "Not necessarily. I'm sure there will be

plenty of that, at first. With time though, they will learn to love their new leader. I will reveal my powers to them, and they will either love me or fear me. It doesn't matter to me which they choose. In the end, I will bend them to my will, and I will save the Earth."

Avani looked over at his comrades; their jaws were slackened, and he knew they felt the same amount of shock as himself. "I knew you were an eccentric, but this is crazy, even for you."

"You call me crazy, but in time you will come to see my way is what's best for Asmaria."

Avani growled, "We won't let you get away with this!"

"Let me?" The man asked, "Who are you to stop me? Look at you. Tied up and useless. Not to mention you couldn't get a single Guild member to take your side. You're all weak, pathetic excuses for leaders."

Avani watched Ember as he strutted away and out of the room. His rage grew with each step. Just before he reached the door, Avani let loose a roar. It was more than a yell. More than a scream. With it, he released every built-up emotion that had been welling inside his mind. The floor shook from the force, causing Ember to look over his shoulder. Was that a flash of fear in his eyes that Avani saw?

Ash climbed from the back of Iguru, excitement, and fear coursing through him in equal parts. His friends were already on the ground. He couldn't contain himself; Ash ran over to Quinn and threw his arms around her. At first, he thought he may have made a mistake, but then she hugged him back and he almost melted. He heard Kane asking Vesta to stay in the area. If something were to happen to them and they did not return, the dragons were to go back to Asmaria and find the Guardians. He wrote a note on a thick piece of paper and wrapped it around her neck with a strip of leather. She snorted steam, which Ash figured was an irritated agreement.

"I was so worried about you back there." He told her.

She chuckled, "Just another Tuesday."

"But today's Thursday." He said, getting another laugh out of her. Seeing her laugh and smile was a magic of its own.

Kane pulled his map back out from his pack and Quinn retrieved the book about Atlantis. Kane said, "It says here that where we're standing is called 'The Eye of The Sahara'. And over here, Atlan says to 'take to the sky and look for the eye'. If this isn't Atlantis then I'll eat my left shoe."

Ash chuckled, "I have a good feeling about this place. But we need to figure out how we're going to find whatever it is that we're looking for. I mean, we don't even know what we're looking for. I don't know if you guys have noticed, but there isn't exactly a whole lot of… well, anything around here."

They looked around them. Quinn said, "You're right. I say we start in the center of the eye and work our way outward. It looks like the center is just right over there." She pointed to a pile of rubble that was just a few meters away.

When they reached the stones, Ash thought that it could have once been part of a man-made structure, but there was no telling how long ago that would have been. They looked around the area, climbed atop the pile of rocks, and searched for any sort of clue. It would have been difficult enough without knowing what it was to look for. The task seemed impossible.

"Okay," Quinn said, "Let's spread out and keep looking now."

Ash climbed down from the rocks and began walking away when he noticed Kane staring at them with his arms crossed. Deep thought seemed to be crinkling his eyebrows. "What is it?" He asked his white-haired friend.

"I feel like there's more to this," was all he said before he started conjuring wind. One by one the boulders were lifted and carefully placed to the side. Ash saw Quinn come back over and watched Kane work. Ash felt bad that he couldn't use lightning to help move boulders out of the way.

After a few minutes, all the rocks were shifted off what appeared to be a small, circular dais made of stone. It had intricate carvings all over and a straight line that split the circle in half. All three studied the dais intently, trying to make sense of it. Finally, Quinn said, "I think it's a lock or a door of some sort."

"What makes you think that?" Kane asked.

"Look at these markings over here. They're runes. I think I can read it a bit."

This girl just kept on surprising Ash. "You can read runes?"

"I've studied many languages. You never know when they might come in handy. These are Atlantean, but they're very similar to others that I've seen before."

Ash asked, "Is there any way we can help decipher them?"

"No. Just give me some time."

After studying the markings for a while she said, "That which crashes and flows will lead the way."

Kane said incredulously, "Wanna explain the riddle, brainiac?"

She squinted her eyes at him, "Well, I don't know for sure, but it sounds like it has something to do with water. Assuming that this was at one point Atlantis, a kingdom floating on the sea, and water *does* have a way of flowing. This whole desert was probably an ocean once; I'm willing to bet water will show us the way."

"There's only one way to find out, water mage." He winked and held out his hands, gesturing for her to try some water magic on the platform.

Quinn looked around a moment more and resigned to trying it on a small bowl-shaped marking near the edge of the structure. She bent down and held out her palm, conjuring water from the air, and filled the bowl to the brim. Nothing happened at first, and then the water began to spread, filling all the carvings in the rock.

The light in the sky was dimming and the lines on the rocky surface began to glow a faint blue as the water spread around. Once the carvings were filled to their entirety, the glowing dissipated and Ash thought it was over. "Well," he said, "that was very anticlimactic." But he spoke too soon.

The crack that ran down the middle of the platform began to slide open. Unfortunately, they were all standing right over the top of it. They tried getting away as the ground opened up, but they weren't quick enough. Kane tripped as he attempted to scramble away, but it was no good. Their screams were drowned out by the roar of the wind as they plummeted into the Earth. As their descent began, Ash saw Kane trying to control the wind. He moved his hands as he normally would, however, the motion did nothing to create any sort of lift beneath them. Ash knew his lightning would be of no help even if it worked but wanted to check. He couldn't create so much as a spark.

They were powerless and falling into darkness. The three of them clung to each other as if that would slow them down. Ash looked down and saw nothing but pitch black and it reminded him of when Aros possessed his body. Fear coursed through him and he wanted nothing more than to curl up in a ball and go to sleep. He glanced upward and already the opening was becoming a speck of yellow.

Trials of Atlantis

It seemed like hours had passed by since their fall through the Earth began. The cold pressed into Ash, gripping him like an icy hand. It was relentless. He held onto his friends, drawing on each other's warmth, as little as it may be. The light above them was completely gone now. There was nothing to be seen. They tried their abilities now and then but it still wouldn't work.

"How long do you think we've been falling?" Ash yelled over the roaring wind of their fall.

Kane yelled back, "I'd say about three years, give or take a few."

Even in this horrible situation, Kane was a jokester. Ash was thankful that at least one of them could remain light-hearted about it all. In the time he'd gotten to him, Kane was almost always looking at the brighter side of things. However now, Ash couldn't see how Kane could be in such high spirits. There was no brighter side to this abyss.

"If we don't make it," Quinn started, "I just want you to know. I love you." Ash's heart threatened to leap out of his chest. And then she said, "Both of you."

What was that supposed to mean? Ash didn't think it was

possible to get colder, and yet here he was, feeling like his temperature dropped twenty degrees. He couldn't tell where their relationship stood. Were they just friends or more? He'd probably never figure that out. The ridiculousness of his thinking about the relationship status of the girl he liked was almost enough to make him burst into laughter. He didn't know what to say to her. Ash still hadn't quite figured out how to express what he was thinking or feeling when it came to Quinn.

Kane once again saved the day, "We love you too, Quinn. Even if you are a waterhead." A cry of pain came from Kane. Quinn must have hit him.

Finally, after what felt like years of falling, the light beneath them began to glow. "Look!" Quinn yelled. The light became brighter and larger. Soon enough a city began to take shape. They were hurtling toward it at what felt like 200 miles per hour with no sign of slowing down. Ash saw Kane trying to use magic again, a look of panic across his usually stoic face, but to no avail. As they got closer, the city grew into what looked almost the same as the picture of Atlantis in the book. It was a glistening kingdom. From this high up Ash couldn't tell what was producing the light. He knew it couldn't be the sun. There were flickers of blue and orange that were giving the city its glow.

They were only a couple hundred feet away from splatting in the courtyard in front of a massive palace. Suddenly, they slammed into an invisible force that Ash thought a pool of cotton would feel like. It didn't hurt in the slightest, but it slowed their descent all the same. The ground rushed at them and just before Ash hit the ground, his body halted, hovering just above the ground. After floating for a millisecond, they all crashed into the cobblestone courtyard.

Ash couldn't believe they were alive. Some warmth began to trickle back into his limbs as he rolled over to a sitting position. He took some deep breaths as he looked around. His relief was short-lived as he just realized they weren't alone. Looking alarmed, he jumped to his feet as men dressed in armor from head to toe encircled them. Their gold-plated armor glittered in the light that he now noticed was being produced by flames burning in torches all over the place. There were blue lights placed around on buildings and such that seemed to move. He didn't have time to figure out what they were at the moment.

The men lowered menacing-looking spears as they stalked toward them. Ash saw his friends get to their feet as well. They squished into each other in a back-to-back fighting position. Ash saw no way out of this but was determined to go down swinging. Ash decided to make the first move. He lunged for the spear closest to him and instantly found himself looking up at the angry face of the man holding the spear. What just happened?

Ash hopped back up to his feet, this time standing much closer to the man. He pulled his arm back to throw a punch, but before he could release it, the man blurred and was suddenly behind Ash. He spun around but the man was quicker. He grabbed Ash by the wrists and they wrestled for control. In the end, Ash was put into cuffs and his bow had gotten smashed. Ash couldn't figure out how the man moved so fast. Ash was too shocked to notice his friends being cuffed as well. Their gear bags were taken from them as they walked toward the large dwelling.

He had two of the armor-clad men dragging him up the steps to what appeared to be the main palace. "What are you doing?"

He asked them. "Take your hands off me!" Ash was becoming impatient and it only got worse when the soldiers wouldn't answer him. Their grip on his arms was beginning to make him sore already. He deduced that they were supernaturally fast and strong so struggling would do no good. He may need to use his brain to get out of this one, and that worried him.

The grandness of the structure before him left Ash feeling a bit overwhelmed. It was the most beautiful palace he'd ever seen, although, he hadn't seen many palaces in his time. There were remnants of what was once an underwater kingdom all over it. Mystical corals and other plant life were attached to its walls, glowing a brilliant teal with bioluminescence. They seemed to be flourishing even though they were no longer underwater. Ash had to remind himself to shut his mouth.

They entered the palace door—which was at least fifty feet tall—and his awe was replaced with fear. He knew his friends were behind him, but the number of eyes on him made Ash feel like he was alone. On either side of him were Atlanteans dressed in flowing robes of all the colors he could think of. Scattered throughout the crowd were more soldiers with swords strapped to their waist. Ash saw children clinging to the legs of what could only be their parents and that put his mind at ease, but only slightly.

At the end of the chamber were more steps that led up to a throne that looked both inanimate and alive at the same time. The golden surface shifted as if it were an ocean wave and had barnacles around its base. The back of the throne was topped with large spikes with the likeness of a harpoon.

The men holding Ash stopped him and the others brought Quinn and Kane around on either side of him. They were simultaneously knocked to their knees and their cuffs released.

Ash felt a huge wave of relief wash over him as he rubbed his wrists which had already become sore despite only being cuffed for a short time. He remembered being held captive in Asmaria. He hadn't been cuffed like this, but being a prisoner didn't sit well with him.

A door behind the throne that Ash hadn't noticed swung open and immediately all the people in the hall dropped down to one knee with their heads bowed. Ash could hear the shuffle of footsteps and a pinging sound bouncing off the walls every couple of seconds. He thought he should bow his head as the others did but couldn't bring himself to tear his eyes away from the man who appeared. Not only the awe that the man brought with him but the smallest bit of defiance that Ash felt would not allow him to bow.

He was massive, but not in a fat sort of way. More like someone who ate a lot and lifted heavy weights in their spare time. He was like a depiction of the Greek gods. His skin was a light bronze color with runic tattoos covering most of his arms. His eyes had an ocean-blue hue. He looked eerily familiar, although Ash couldn't quite place where he recognized him from. The man appeared to be old and yet had a look of youth about him at the same time. His long brown hair was curly, dusted with flakes of silver, and his beard matched.

Although Ash could tell this was the King, the man didn't dress like most Kings would. He didn't wear a crown, nor have ornate rings on his fingers. He wore a sleeveless, teal shirt that showed off his ripped arms. And his pants were loosely fitting with a dark green color. His brown sandals were the most normal thing Ash could see about him. He held a golden trident in his hand, the metal of it pinging off the hard floor with each stride he took.

The presence that the man before him commanded was immense. He possessed a great power that was palpable. The people only lifted their heads and arose once the King was seated upon his throne. Ash heard Quinn gasp as she lifted her head and saw him for the first time.

When he spoke, Ash felt soothed by the Atlantean accent that rolled off his tongue. It was unlike anything he'd ever heard before. His voice was deep and reverberated off the chamber walls. "You have entered the kingdom of Atlantis without permission. You there," he pointed at Ash. "State your business here."

Ash tried to gulp down the knot that had formed in his throat. "Sir, we come from the land of Asmaria. We came in search of something to save the Great Tree—the uh, source of power that keeps the island and our magic alive—and we have reason to believe that it's here."

The King's face remained unreadable, although he seemed to be mulling over what Ash told him. "Something to save this tree, hmm? What is this 'something'?"

Ash chuckled, "Well, that's the thing. We're not sure what it could be. She told us—"

"She?" The King interrupted.

"Yes, sir. The Great Tree is mysterious to most of us, especially me. I don't know all of its secrets, but the Tree revealed her original identity to me in a vision. She told me her name is Gethin." The King shifted in his seat at that.

"How do I know what you say is true?" he asked.

Before Ash could respond, Kane said, "Please, sir. We've given you no reason to find us untrustworthy."

The King stood from his throne slowly and said, "Oh? How about entering my kingdom without permission? How about attacking my sentries upon arrival?"

"That was just a big misunderstanding!" Ash could hear the irritation in Kane's voice and worried that things were about to get ugly.

Kane didn't wait for a response before he began, "Look—" but the King slammed the butt of his trident on the floor. The sound cut him off and rang out through the hall. Ash's stomach jumped back up into his throat. The look in the man's eyes made Ash want to run.

He sauntered down the steps to where they kneeled and stopped in front of Kane. "Rise." He told him. Kane did as he was ordered and stood. He was only a foot away from the King and was a whole head shorter. The King took a step back and, in a flash, put both hands on the trident. He thrust the three-pronged weapon towards Kane's throat. Ash's breath caught as everything happened both in slow motion and too fast for him to react. Luckily, Kane was always ready; before the trident's tines could pierce his skin, he reached behind his back and pulled out two karambits, one in each hand.

Kane was able to block the trident with the curved blades just inches from his throat. Ash could see his arms shaking from the strain. Ash looked to Quinn whose eyes were wide with what could only be fear. Ash became angry. How could this lunatic not see that they were there with good intentions? And why were they so powerless here? He couldn't just sit here and watch his best friend get skewered.

The time for thinking about anything had passed and it was time to act. Ash jumped to his feet and came flying in, kicking the trident away from Kane. He whirled around and tried swinging at the King. The man easily dodged his strike and swung the trident around, smacking him in the stomach with the butt end. Ash doubled over and, in his peripherals, saw Quinn come running in, throwing a combo of her own. She was knocked to the ground with a swift kick to the sternum.

Kane charged, swinging his karambits in a deadly flurry of metal that would have left almost anyone dead. The King, however, was quicker than he looked. Ash saw him dodge every attack and then put Kane on the ground as well. Only then did he gesture for backup from his soldiers. They were swarmed once again and this time checked for weapons after being cuffed.

"Take them to the holding cells," Ash heard the King command. "Let's see how a few days of solitary does them.

The first thing the sentries did was split the three kids up. Ash's cuffs were released and he was tossed in a dirty holding cell. His dusty cell let him know that it had been some time since anyone had been held there. He was almost fourteen years old and had been imprisoned twice in his life now. Both within a couple of days of each other.

The sounds coming from inside this particular prison were excruciating to the ears. It was a mix of screams, moans, and mumbling voices that made no sense. The incoherent speeches were filling Ash's head. He did his best to block them out.

Ash tried to conjure lightning and he still couldn't produce the tiniest bit. Something about this place was blocking their magic, that he was certain of. This prison was unlike the one back in Asmaria; it had three walls made of stone and the entrance was steel bars running from floor to ceiling. He couldn't see anything from right to left on the outside of his cell. There was no way of knowing where his friends had been taken or if they were even still alive.

He had been hungry before, but not like this. Ash found

himself ready to start gnawing at his hand at any second. Luckily for him and his hand, after what had to have been days, he was taken from the cell. They didn't bother to put cuffs on him this time, which he thought was smart. There was no way he had enough energy to fight off anyone.

The guards took him to a small building not far from the main palace. He could see it in the background behind what looked like a city hall of some sort. There were runes above the entrance and he felt a pang of longing for Quinn. She was the only one in their group who could read these. Ash wished she were with him, but not only to read the inscription.

Once inside the building, he was taken to a circular room. It didn't look much different from the auditorium in the Guild building but it was much smaller. Ash counted five people aside from the guards who were milling about. He was sat in a chair with two other empty ones. They didn't say anything to him and when Ash tried to ask a question, he was adamantly shushed.

Within a few minutes, Quinn and Kane were walked inside as well and Ash was relieved to see them. In the past several months he had never been separated from them for such a long period. He tried talking to them but was shushed again. Ash didn't like to be shushed.

The King entered the arena and, again, everyone took a knee and bowed their heads. Ash and his friends all followed suit this time. There was a large stone chair near the other five Atlanteans where the King sat.

"You have been brought here today," the King said, "to stand trial for your crimes."

Crimes? What crimes? Their intentions were good and Ash was determined to prove it to him. If this was a trial then surely they would allow the kids to defend themselves. Ash couldn't wrap his mind around how he was on trial *again.*

A man in dark blue robes entered the chamber. He looked menacing. He held a small wooden box in his hands with runes carved into it. Ash heard Quinn audibly gasp and swiveled his head to her. He lifted his eyebrows in a gesture to ask what was wrong, but she merely shook her head.

The man laid the box down on a table and withdrew its contents. To Ash, it just looked like a couple of vials of a translucent white liquid. Whatever it was, it couldn't be good. The man creepily walked over to them, grabbing Ash by the hair on the back of his head. He wrenched his head back, "Open," he commanded. Ash was getting scared at this point, so he just did as he was told. A couple of drops of the fluid hit his tongue and slid down his throat.

It didn't have much of a taste and what he could taste wasn't too bad. A weird feeling settled over him, his brain felt foggy. Warmth spread from his throat, down to his stomach, and out to his fingertips. He didn't even notice that Quinn and Kane were subjected to the liquid as well.

The King's words were muffled now but Ash could just barely make out what was being said, "You are now under our truth serum. Even if you wanted to lie, the pain would be too excruciating. So you may as well tell us what we want to know."

The people who were first gathered there arose from their seats and walked over to stand in front of the kids. Four of the five were men with gray hair and beards, the last was a woman with equally gray hair. They spoke in unison as if they were of one mind. Their jumble of voices was discomforting to Ash, "We are the Elders. The eldest of our race. You will answer each question with candor, or die."

Ash didn't want to die. He didn't plan on lying to them. The first question they asked was, "What is your name?" Ash took the lead by telling them his name and then the other two did the same. *As long as our stories match, we'll get through this,* Ash groggily thought.

"How did you find this place?" The Elders croaked out.

Ash answered, "From a book called 'Mythical Lands From A-Z.'" The elders continued to stare at them so Ash added, "There was a… section about Atlantis. That is where we are right? Well, anyway, in that section there was a note from… from…" Ash was blanking on the name and his head was beginning to hurt, causing him to grimace. Quinn jumped in, "It was from King Atlan."

Ash's headache disappeared and the fog returned. "Right, thanks. King Atlan said in the note that he feared Atlantis would soon be destroyed. He said to… to take to the sky and look for the eye. And so, here we are!" Ash chuckled.

The elders looked between each other and nodded, "What is your purpose for trespassing in our kingdom?"

"Well," Kane said, "that's a bit of a long story."

"We have all the time in the world." The Elders each smiled slyly.

"So," Kane started again, "we have this tree in the land we come from—"

"And which land is that?"

"Asmaria. We have this tree, we call it the Great Tree by the way, and the Great Tree is the source of our power. I'd show you how truly amazing I am, but for some… reason, my powers haven't worked since we fell through that hole."

"Wait," Ash interrupted, "I already told them about the Tree.

Well… I told that guy." Ash pointed at the man with the trident.

"Young man," the elders said, "do not test our patience. What you're saying has nothing to do with what brought you here, and *that man* just so happens to be our King. Show some respect."

"Allow me to help," Quinn said. "So, the Great Tree was attacked many… months ago. She's dying. She gave all of us Asmarians a vision, telling us that we would find the key to her survival in the kingdom once lost at sea. Naturally, many of us thought of… Atlantis. Although, your kingdom has been a myth to everyone until now."

"Final question," the Elders said. "Why should we trust you? Even if what you say is true. Why should we help you?"

Ash thought for a moment. That was a good question. "Because it's the right thing to do. When other people… are in need of help. The good thing to do is to help if you have the ability."

The elders seemed to be out of questions for they turned to the King. He motioned for them to take their seats and they complied. The King stood and said, "I've heard enough." And then he banged his trident on the floor. Ash saw a shockwave ripple out and as it passed over him, the fog lifted from his mind.

"Asmarians, welcome to Atlantis. I am King Gabriel." He smiled widely.

The gears in Ash's brain were turning. Gabriel was the same name as the statue back at the Capital. The one who was supposedly Asmaria's first Guardian. Was this the same man? He didn't have to think on it long, Quinn's brilliant mind did the work for him.

"You were once an Asmarian, weren't you?" She said, her

eyes narrowing.

He laughed, "You're the bright one of the bunch I presume. I could sense that you suspected something like that from the start, or am I wrong?"

She chuckled, "No, you're correct, sir. I recognized you from the statue."

His eyes widened, "Statue? There's a statue of me?"

"Yeah," Ash said, "Right in the middle of the Capital. I thought you looked familiar, but I had no idea where it could have been from."

"So," Kane interjected, "about why we came."

"Oh, there will be plenty of time for that, my boy. Let's get you kids some food first. Yeah?"

Ash lit up, the fog in his brain beginning to lift at that sentence. "Those are the greatest words I've heard in my whole time here!"

Stone of Ruin

Augustus searched high and low for the Stone of Ruin. This particular mystical artifact had been lost for thousands of years. But Aros, his dark master, would lead him to it. Aros had lost the battle against the Asmarians, even with Ash's body. Aros had underestimated them—and most of all—Ash's ability to fight the mind control enacted by the dark lord as he possessed the boy.

Now, Aros rested in their new lair. The only logical thing to do after losing that battle was to flee and recover. They would come back stronger this time, never to be embarrassed by them again. The demon king had been with Augustus for such a long time that he now felt naked without him in his head. The pure power that fed into his body when Aros possessed him was so addictive, and now his drug had been taken away from him.

He hadn't always been this way; Augustus was once on the path to being a Guardian, but those days were long gone now. Aros came into his life and showed him a different way to power. Sure, there were a few sacrifices he had to make in the beginning, but he didn't think about it much anymore. At first, he had regretted killing his wife. But in the end, Aros' way would lead to prosperity for those who follow him.

Augustus was climbing through the Swiss Alps with his new right-hand man, Draven. Draven was young and malleable, being close to adulthood. His mind was fit for molding. This is where Aros told them the stone could be found. They would know it by the power wafting from it.

"What's this stone supposed to do, my Lord? I mean, it's just a rock, right?" Draven asked.

If Aros had been occupying his body, Augustus probably would have had an outburst of anger at the question. However, with his mind being his own, his temperament was much more forgiving. "I don't know the specifics. All I know is that Lord Aros ordered us to find it and that it will ensure he wins the coming war against the Asmarians."

"Not one for giving up details, is he?"

Augustus chuckled, "That he is not. You do see that the cause is just, don't you?"

Augustus sensed hesitation in the young man, "Well, sir, I was raised in the Forbidden. All I've known is the shadows my whole life. Now that I'm grown and can make my own choices, I'm not sure. I know that's not what you wanted to hear but- "

"You're right." He said, "It's not. And don't you let anyone else hear you say that? If Aros was possessing me right now, you would be flung from this mountain. I've grown a liking for you, so I don't want to see that happen. Got it?"

"Yes. It won't happen again." There was a brief silence between them before Draven said, "What convinced you to fight on his side?"

Augustus remembered the night that Aros came to him. "Aros visited me in a dream. He showed me the true evils of the world. The other humans, they don't value the Earth or life like we do. They don't see anything as sacred except for their most selfish desires. Most people in this world will stab their best friend in the back if it propels them higher. Aros gave me a vision of what our world would come to if I didn't help him overcome the danger that is humanity. In the end, this planet will be left in ruins if we do nothing.

"The Asmarians consider themselves to be the heroes and we the villains, while they sit idly by and leave the rest of the world to its own devices. They refuse to interfere in the rest of the world's antics. This is a folly. I do the things I do for my fellow Asmarians because I too was one of them. I will be the one to save them from themselves whether they want me to or not."

Through his labored breaths, Draven said, "Well, if what you say is true, then I'm on board as well. And I do believe you are being truthful. I just wish…" he paused.

"Wish what, Draven?"

"I wish that it was easier. I wish we didn't have to live in the darkness to thrive. I wish that Aros wasn't such an evil being. Whether he's trying to save the world or not, to his core, he is vile. But like I said, I'm on board."

Augustus stopped climbing and turned to Draven, "Everything spoken here stays between us." He feared what would happen if Aros searched his memories and found this conversation. Draven nodded in agreement, and they continued.

They were nearing the top when Augustus finally reached a semi-flat part. He stood up, breathing warm air over his freezing fingers. The cold mountain air whipped around his black cloak. And then he saw it. It was like a whisp of black smoke flitted past his eyes. He turned, and a trail of the faintest black mist appeared to be curling around the side of the mountain.

"This way, hurry." He ordered his sidekick.

They scurried around the corner of the rock, their backs pressed tightly against the face of the mountain and their feet scooting across the narrow ledge. As they went further around, the black whisp became clearer. Augustus made it to another flat platform and found the mouth of a rather small cave. He would have to crawl through it.

"It has to be in there. Do you see the trail?" Augustus asked.

"I do," Draven answered, bright-eyed.

Augustus dropped down to his hands and knees, igniting a ball of fire in his hand. He thrust it forward, sending the fireball hurtling through the cave. It seemed to be a rather long tunnel; his flame dissipated before it reached the end. They began crawling through.

Luckily, it was too cold for anything to live up here. Otherwise, Augustus figured there would have been a heavy surplus of spiders in that tunnel. It took several minutes to make it through, but when they did, it opened up to a large chamber. Augustus kept his hands aflame so they could see. Stalactites were hanging from the tall ceiling and in the middle of the chamber was a cylindrical table protruding from the rocky floor. Sitting dead center was a stone in the shape of a pyramid. It was black like obsidian and, in the firelight, had a bluish tint to it. He recalled Aros telling him something of the Stone of Ruin. It was imbued with dark magic thousands of years ago. The relic was used in wars long before mankind was born into existence.

Augustus approached the stone slowly, being cautious. It almost seemed too easy to him. There had to be a trap somewhere. He refused to make it this far just to fall victim to a silly boobytrap. He increased his flames to make the chamber brighter. He couldn't see anything nefarious about it, but that's what made him uneasy. He was now just a few inches away from the stone. He reached out and gripped it gently, pulling it off the table. Nothing happened at first, but a second later the ceiling and walls began closing in.

"Go!" He shouted to Draven. They bolted for the tiny cave opening. Draven jumped into the hole and Augustus made it just in time. The ceiling behind them clipped his cloak and he had to give it a hard tug to free it. The two of them crawled back out the way they'd come.

Augustus turned the stone over in his hands, eyeing it with curiosity. He wondered about it just as much as Draven, but he knew when to ask Aros questions and when to just do as he was told.

"I guess we get to go back home now," Draven said. Augustus thought he detected a hint of disappointment in his voice.

He told the young man, "Don't get down. With this, the tides will be turned in our favor. The war will be over before you know it."

Augustus thought of Draven as the son he never got to raise. One of the only things he still regretted to this day was having to abandon Ash on that park bench. Aros made it known that it would be necessary to leave him so that he would develop his powers properly. All that was left to do now was return the Stone to the obelisk so that Aros would be able to increase his power. Once everything is done, Aros' promise to him will finally be fulfilled.

To The Lab

The dinner the Atlanteans put on for Ash and his friends was nothing short of a feast. There was a smorgasbord of things Ash could only imagine. He didn't know what most of it was and hoped it wasn't anything weird, although, most of it tasted phenomenal. There was some sort of brown goopy thing that almost made him hurl the contents of his stomach. After dinner, King Gabriel took them to the amphitheater where they watched a show put on by dancers. Ash already felt like he was learning so much about their culture and he loved it.

Upon traveling around the kingdom, Ash noticed that the city was surrounded by rock. It truly had been swallowed up by the Earth. The rocky walls on the outskirts were covered in bioluminescent creatures which cast a soft blue glow over the city. It was enough to make it easy to see everything. The flamed torches that were scattered around everywhere certainly helped as well. Those flames never seemed to dull or die out.

Atlantis was still mysterious; Ash didn't know how they got their food or survived down here. He wasn't able to ask Gabriel about much of anything yet. He just hoped they would find what they came here for and be able to return to Asmaria in time.

"So," Ash began, "how do you guys keep track of time down here? With there being no sunlight or modern technology, I can't help but be curious about it all."

Gabriel said, "Time is not something our people have to worry about."

Ash didn't feel like that answered his question. This man was an enigma.

Quinn asked, "King Gabriel, how is it that you're still alive? The statue of you in Asmaria is hundreds of years old, at least."

He chuckled, "As I said before, we don't have to worry about time here. The magic that protects our kingdom makes us impervious to old age. We're not exactly immortal. Natural illness and other causes of death still apply to us. But we will not die from old age. I just happen to be lucky enough to not have yet perished from disease, and well, down here we don't exactly have to worry about being attacked."

"How did you guys end up here? The book we told you about was purely theoretical. No one in history has had solid evidence about Atlantis' existence or how the kingdom fell." Kane asked.

Gabriel's eyes seemed to darken, "I will tell you everything you wish to know. However, it's better if I have some wine in me before I begin." The King led them to a building with runes over the entrance that Quinn translated to Ash, 'Banquet Hall'. They all sat at a long, rectangular table made of a light blue stone. Several servants appeared and began dishing out drinks to them. Ash wondered if they were giving them wine but when he looked at the liquid in his goblet, it was a dark blue color. He took a drink, and it was fizzy like soda and tasted like raspberries.

"Now then," King Gabriel said, "where were we? Ah, yes, my kingdom's history. Please, feel free to interrupt with questions along the way. I can be rather long-winded. Atlantis was born thousands of years ago. Before Asmaria even. And yet, we've only known three rulers in that time. My father, Atlan, my elder brother, Thaidan, and myself. I believe your people know me as the first Guardian, which I guess is true in a way, although, things were different back then."

Gabriel paused for a moment, seemingly deep in thought, and then continued. Gesturing to Ash, "You mentioned the name Gethin back in my throne room. I once knew her. When she was alive in her original form. I'm assuming that's the form she took when she revealed herself to you."

Ash was surprised. He remembered the King seemed to recognize the name, but he didn't think to consider it as a possibility.

"Back in the days of old when we lived at the surface amongst the sea, our shaman predicted a massive earthquake that would cast us into oblivion. I searched the world for many years, looking for anything that might save us apart from relocating. That's when I found Asmaria. Back then, the people were powerless. They welcomed me in with open arms."

Ash interrupted, "Sir, why not just relocate? Wouldn't that have been easier?"

"Aye, it's possible that it would have been easier, for a time at least. With our magic and riches, we were often the target of attacks from other societies. At the time, we thought it best to look for other avenues.

"The fairy folk of Asmaria used to outnumber the humans there and Gethin was their Queen. She was the most powerful being I had ever met. Even then, we Atlanteans had abilities that surpassed most other humans on Earth. Gethin was a whole different entity. She could create the most beautiful things in life, and destroy them just as easily.

"She became my best friend before long. I helped train the Asmarians so they could protect their home. The thing about humans is, that no matter who they are or where they're located, someone out there wants what they have. Asmaria was no different. I turned them into warriors and created the Guild. The Guardians were formed to lead the Guild into battle, so naturally, I was the first Guardian."

Kane asked him, "If Gethin was once a fairy, what happened?"

The King leaned forward, resting his forearms on the table. "Tragedy happened. There was a vile demon who sought nothing but power for himself. His ultimate goal was world domination. He somehow knew of Gethin and wanted to destroy her and take her power for himself. He attacked, bringing with him a horde of people he'd corrupted. They were no longer human at that point. Gethin allowed each Asmarian to have a portion of her power and together, we defeated the beast. However, this wasn't before he dealt a fatal blow to Gethin. In her dying moments, she cast a spell that turned her into a tree. She was already nearly immortal before the spell."

Ash looked to both of his friends and, by the expressions they wore, they were all thinking the same thing. "Did the demon's name happen to be Aros?" Ash asked.

"Yes. So you've heard of him?"

"I don't know how to explain any of this, but you should know, he's back."

Gabriel's face paled, "What do you mean, he's back? He can't be. I watched him die!" He seemed to be getting angry.

"Like I said," Ash said, "I can't explain it. All I know is, he's the reason we're here. Aros is killing Gethin. The Great Tree is dying, and she sent us here to retrieve something key to her survival. Of course, she didn't tell us what to look for."

Gabriel laughed, "Same old Gethin. She loves her riddles. Shortly after she turned into the tree, I would often visit and speak to her. I didn't think she was still alive in that form. Then one day I was talking to her, and a branch reached down and wrapped around me. She gave me a vision with a riddle and with that, we were able to create the spell that keeps this place together. It would seem her wisdom increased sevenfold after her ascension. The earthquake happened and we fell into the Earth. The sea sank into the ground and our city remained mostly intact. Tell me the exact riddle she gave you and I may be able to help."

Quinn, being the brainy one, told him the riddle. Gabriel rested his chin on a closed fist and thought about the riddle for a few minutes. They sat there in silence until he said, "I don't claim to be the smartest man amongst my people, however, I think I know where to start."

They got up and followed him out of the building. As they walked down the street, Ash saw children playing with a small ball. They were running around, laughing giddily. He was enjoying his time here and thought that it wouldn't be the worst thing in the world if they had to stay. Having that thought made him feel guilty. He couldn't just leave the Asmarians to be killed by Aros. Gethin said that the demon grew stronger. He would be a much more formidable foe this time. The silence from the Forbidden since the battle left Ash concerned.

Gabriel led them to a small structure that he said was their spell lab. It's where they experiment with different spells and elixirs. He explained that the spell that was keeping them safe had some conditions along with it. Once entering the spell's range, they would not be able to reenter Atlantis if they leave. The spell deadens all mystical abilities, which explains why Ash and his friends were unable to wield magic. Their shaman had found a way around this which is why their guards were so fast. They'd been given a spell that allowed them to have superhuman speed and strength but didn't alter the integrity of the original spell.

The King spoke with his shaman in the lab about their problem. Ash turned to his comrades and said, "This is unbelievable. I mean, I believe him, I don't have a reason not to. But it would seem that some of the Asmarian history is incorrect."

Quinn said, "Did you see his face when you told him that Aros was still alive? He got so angry. I wish we could convince him to help us fight, but I know that won't happen. He wouldn't doom his kingdom just to help us. And if any of the Atlanteans lived they wouldn't be able to return to their home."

"I know one thing," Kane said. "I want to get my hands on that superhuman spell. I mean, I know everyone already sees me as a superhuman, but let's be honest, those guards were faster than me."

Ash punched him on the arm playfully and said, "You only think that because I'm always letting you win our sparring matches."

"Oh yeah?" Kane responded, getting into a fighting stance. "You want to go at it right here?" The boys began to circle each other, chuckling.

Quinn grabbed them each by an ear, "That's enough, boys.

Don't embarrass me." She let go and Ash rubbed his throbbing ear.

"No need to be so mean," Kane said.

Ash agreed, "Yeah." Then he blew a raspberry at her to which she just rolled her eyes.

Gabriel walked back over to them and said, "I think we will be able to help you. It's going to take some time, but I'm confident that we can find a solution that will work."

"How much time?" Quinn asked.

"That I don't know. It could be anywhere from a couple of days to a couple of months."

"We don't have months." Ash said, "But there's nothing else we can do. We just need to have faith that we will get back in time."

Kane asked, "What are we going to do with all this free time? What do the Atlanteans do for fun around here?"

The King smiled widely and chuckled, "I thought you'd never ask!"

Enter Delirium

Avani couldn't believe that he'd let himself get captured so easily. He felt that he and the others could have defeated the other Guild members, but it wouldn't have been without bloodshed. They were able to keep from killing anyone but at the price of being captured, their hands bound so they couldn't wield magic. Now they were sitting in front of the Guild for 'judgment', or so Ember called it. It would seem the psychopath felt the other Guardians deserved to be punished for their so-called treason.

"Fellow mages." Ember began, "As most of you are aware, we are gathered here today for the judgment of the other Guardians. Avani, Bora, and Leena are all being tried for treason. They were witnessed by, not just me, but many of you in aiding those three brats in escaping Asmaria. With them, they took three of our dragons and countless other items that should stay here."

Ember turned to the three Guardians. "How do you plead?"

The three looked between one another and Leena said, "Not guilty, *obviously.*"

Ember smirked and then turned to the crowd. "Guild members. Those in favor of finding the accused party in question guilty, please raise your hand." More hands went up than Avani could count. "And now those who vote not guilty." Hands went up again, but Avani could already tell that the guilty voters outweighed the other. Even if their supporter was slim, Avani was thankful that a few had their backs in this situation.

Avani was starting to panic. With their hands bound so tightly, there was nothing they could do. They need a little bit of space to wield magic and like this, they would be doomed to suffer whatever punishment Ember could come up with. Avani strained against the bindings, but it was futile; the ropes were too thick for him to break.

He stood up, doing the only thing he could think of. "My people, listen to me! You mustn't fall for this! Those children were not traitors, and neither are we!" He paused, an attempt at letting his words take a dramatic effect. "Ember has gone off the deep end. Accusing kids of being in allegiance with the Forbidden. Trying to kill the Great Tree. And now imprisoning his fellow Guardians. Can't you see? He will stop at nothing to attain power, that's all he cares about. Stop this madness!"

Avani was met with nothing but silence. Then Ember broke it with a chuckle, "Well, that was certainly… entertaining. Is there anyone here that wants to save these three?"

No one stood. No one spoke up for them. Avani could see downcast eyes as he scanned the crowd, utterly desperate for someone to support them. And then it came. A man stood in the front row. Avani knew that his name was Marcus. He was a fellow earth mage.

Marcus climbed over the railing and down onto the floor where the Guardians were. He walked over to Ember, "You've lost your mind, Ember. There's no way they have committed treason. I was on the fence about the kids too. Either way, I don't agree with your methods in the slightest. I'm going to free them." And then he walked over to Avani.

Avani watched as Ember moved behind Marcus silently. "Look out—" he began, but it was too late. A flaming sword exploded through Marcus' chest, stopping a few inches from Avani's face. The flame disappeared and the light fled from the man's eyes. He dropped dead at Avani's feet. His shoes would have been soaked in blood had the flaming sword not cauterized the wound. Ember's eyes were glowing orange as he seethed at Avani.

"See what you caused by your outburst?" He said and then turned to the other Guild members. "Anyone else care to step out of line?" And of course, this time, no one did.

Avani felt pure rage radiate through his body. He would break free of whatever bond this maniac could come up with, and he would end him in the most violent way he could conjure. This was his vow.

"What do we do now?" Bora asked the other two.

"Not much we can do but wait," Avani said. "Let's hope the kids return before we starve to death. We certainly aren't going anywhere."

"That's not the optimistic Avani that I've come to know and love." Leena joked.

At least someone still has a sense of humor, Avani thought.

"I don't have any optimism. But I do have hope and trust in Ash. He pulled through for us last time. We just have to believe that he'll do it again." Avani truly believed what he said.

Leena said, "I guess we should try and get comfy then."

Avani knew there would be no pleasantness given to them

in their current state. Not like this. He leaned back against the wall, the heavy concrete that trapped his hands lying on his thighs. It was hard like a rock, but it wasn't something he could control. He closed his eyes and laid his head against the hard wall behind him, a feeble attempt at gaining some level of comfortability.

Avani wasn't certain of how many days had passed, but he could guess it was at least a week since they'd been thrown into the cell. No food or water had been presented to them since then, and no one had come to check on them. There was a lonely flame flickering in one corner, casting dim light around the chamber. Every so often, a jungle mouse would scurry nearby and each time, Avani would feel his mouth begin to water.

He could hear a scuffle going on outside; he desperately hoped it was some food. He looked between his comrades. They at least needed water. How cruel it was that there was a water mage in their midst with no power to conjure that which could help them survive.

A door crashed open, and a man was flung into their cell. "What is going on here? Where is Ash?" The man demanded.

"Welcome, Rick Hampton," Avani said. Rick spun around wildly. He squatted down and grabbed Avani by the front of his green tunic gently.

"Don't worry, Avani. I'm here to help."

Avani smiled deliriously, "You joined our little party, man."

"Snap out of it!" Rick clapped his hands in front of Avani's face to snap him out of his stupor.

"Sorry," Avani said. "It's been what, a week since we got tossed down here?"

Rick shook his head. "It's been nearly three weeks. Ash

vanished without so much as a goodbye, so I got worried. I started asking around but no one would answer my questions. It wasn't until I went to the Averys—Quinn's parents—and asked if they knew what was going on. They were very reluctant to talk to me about it, but I eventually wore them down."

Avani was surprised at how fast time could slip away down here. "Three weeks. I can't believe it. Well," he looked to the other Guardians, "I guess we'll all be dead pretty soon."

"I'm not going to let that happen," Rick told them. "After finding out what happened to our kids and then you guys, we've developed a plan. I went to Ember and threatened him with everything in me to tell me what was happening, and he had me arrested and brought here. Don't worry though, it's all part of the plan. Believe it or not, there are still a few mages in the Guild who support your side. It seems they just got too scared to speak out. We're gonna bust the three of you out of here. Although, no one realized your hands were stuck in cement. That complicates things. We'll have to bust that apart before we move you. It's not going to be easy. It may break your hands."

"I can't speak for my friends here," Bora said, "but you break every little bone in my hands if that's what it takes to free me."

Avani said, "Me too."

"Same here."

The Atlanteum

Kane knew there had to be something to do around this giant, underground city. The Atlanteans were in great physical condition and, despite living like mole people, in very high spirits. There were some grumblers here and there that he noticed, but for the most part, the people had a positive outlook on life. He thought to himself if he lived down here all these years, he would have to find *some* way to keep himself entertained.

King Gabriel had them riding in chariots pulled by the strangest-looking horses Kane had ever seen. He hadn't seen many, only paintings really, but these were vastly different. They appeared to be around the same size, but they all had brown fur with teal lines all over their bodies. The teal glowed brightly and would get even brighter when the horses were happy or content.

Kane was with Gabriel while Ash and Quinn rode in a chariot together. *Go figure,* he thought. The more he sees the two of them together, the more he wants to find a girlfriend of his own. He knew that they hadn't made it official or anything, but who were they kidding? A blind man with a paper sack over his head could tell that they liked each other. Kane wasn't necessarily jealous of Ash for being with Quinn, he was just jealous of their relationship in general. But that wasn't important at the time. Kane put his jealous feelings into the compartment where he stored every other ugly emotion and locked it tight.

The magic here was very strange to Kane. It was as if the entire city of Atlantis had fallen into the Earth and pushed that which was under it straight into the ground. They appeared to be nearing the edge of the city because, in front of them, Kane could see rock walls ascending into the darkness above. The bioluminescent creatures that covered almost everything didn't go farther than a couple hundred feet up the wall.

Built into the face of the rock was a structure that was derivative of the famous Roman Coliseum. This one looked like it had been carved from the rock, rather than dropping down with the rest of the kingdom.

Gabriel elbowed Kane to get his attention and said, "Magnificent, isn't it?" Kane could see a gleam in his eye.

"It looks just like the Roman Coliseum, only… smaller." He hoped he hadn't offended the man.

Gabriel didn't sound angry when he said, "Well who do you think helped the Romans build the Coliseum in the first place?" He laughed loudly when Kane's eyes grew larger with bewilderment.

"What exactly do you do in there?" Kane asked, remembering what he'd read about the Romans and their arena battles. If it was anything like that, then they were in deeper trouble than he originally thought.

"Nothing like those barbaric Romans." He placed his thumb and index finger on his chin, "Well, I wouldn't say *nothing* like them." He smirked, not revealing anything more to Kane.

The horses came to a stop, and they all dismounted. Kane

couldn't tell whether he was nervous or excited. He decided to at least pretend like it was excitement. If it was nervousness, perhaps his brain would trick itself into perceiving it as being excited and he'd be able to thrive in whatever environment he was about to be thrust into. He was a good fighter, great even, but he'd almost always had the power of his wind magic to rely upon. Gabriel turned and waited for the other two to catch up. Ash and Quinn were gawking at the edifice before them.

"This is what I like to call, 'The Atlanteum'. This is where we do battle, similar to what the Romans used to do. However, we don't kill each other for sport here. It's simply a tournament of friendly fights to see who the best warrior is. While we wait for our shaman to come up with a solution for you, we will have a little competition to see what you three are made of. I'm dying to know what makes an Asmarian mage these days."

"But sir," Quinn said, "doesn't it seem a bit unfair to test our abilities when we don't have our magic?"

The King responded, "That's the best part, my dear. This arena was shaped from the rock you see behind it. Our wards falter past the doorway. You will have all your natural power to help you in battle. But be warned; I've been very friendly and cordial with you up to this point. If you, for whatever reason, decide to betray my kindness, I won't hesitate to end you."

The look in Gabirel's eyes told him that he wasn't joking around. "Now then," the King said, "who's ready to fight?"

There were no doors, just a massive, gaping hole in the outer wall of the Atlanteum. Kane had only seen paintings in books of the Roman Coliseum and from what he remembered, they looked eerily similar. It did appear to be much smaller than the original, and from what he could tell there weren't any trap doors in the ground that would send wild animals bursting out to devour any of them.

There were hundreds of people in the crowd, already cheering. It seemed that the entire kingdom had shown up for today's events. Emblazoned sconces scattered around the arena gave it enough light to see and fight in. There were already several warriors gathered around with an assortment of weapons. There were tables with knives, racks that held swords, and barrels filled with spears and poleaxes.

"So, what are the rules?" Kane asked, turning back to Gabriel.

"I think today we will do a little one-on-one, tournament style, and see who takes it all. Sound fair?" The King had a smug look on his face.

"Well, I would suggest getting more than one of these guys to go against me," Kane said. "If you want them to have any sort of chance at winning that is."

King Gabriel threw his head back with laughter, "I love the confidence, my boy. I'll make you a deal. If you win it all, I'll give you all the gold you can dream of. Down here it's merely used for trading goods amongst the shopkeepers, but on the surface, I'm sure it has much greater value."

"Okay," he said, "just don't get mad when I take all your money." The King gave another chuckle.

He doesn't understand who he's dealing with, Kane thought.

Kane and the other two looked through the inventory of weapons. Kane was searching for throwing stars or something similar. They were his favorite weapon—and his strongest—but they weren't all he was good with. His search came up empty and, in the end, he settled for a pair of daggers. Kane found a couple of thigh sheaths for them and strapped them on. He tried on some armor but it was too bulky and heavy, so he decided to not use it. It seemed Ash and Quinn felt the same way; none of them were accustomed to wearing armor.

"Atlanteans!" The King called out, his voice calming down the bustling of the crowd. "Please assist me in welcoming our guests from Asmaria." The gathered people cheered louder than before and jumped up and down in their seats.

He continued, "The tournament will get started shortly. If the Asmarians win, I will gift them a large lump of gold that would make them very rich on the surface. However, *when* we win, I will grant the winner a free pass to be King for a day. Now then, are you ready?" The crowd became even louder. "Begin!"

The tournament began with Kane fighting a man who appeared to be a bit older, but they were relatively the same size. The man's hair was greying, but other than that he looked to be in great physical shape. His muscles were more defined than Kanes, his limbs not quite as lanky. He was wearing tight, emerald-green pants and had a sword reminiscent of the Roman gladius strapped to his waist. There was a round shield strapped to his non-dominant arm. Kane made a mental note to not let the man get too close.

Somewhere in the arena, the deep tone of a bass drum rumbled out, denoting the start of the match. The man wasted no time; he ripped his sword from its scabbard and charged at Kane, letting loose a battle cry. Kane felt his magic coursing through him. It had been too long since he'd conjured it and only at that moment did he realize how much he'd missed it. He thrusted his palms toward the ground and a gust of wind lifted him, just as the tip of his opponent's sword was about to impale him.

He hovered just out of the man's reach, wiggling his fingers at him as he looked up from the ground. His look of confusion brought Kane joy and he blew a raspberry at him. The man then jumped with what could only be explained as super strength. His vertical leap was at least five feet. He reached Kane's ankle effortlessly and pulled him back to the ground. Kane landed on his back, and the wind forced out from his lungs. He gasped as the warrior placed the tip of his blade to Kane's throat and said, "Yield."

Kane knew he had to be quick if he wanted to win. His confidence would not allow him to lose the first match. He nodded his head as if he were about to yield, but then he grabbed a dagger from his sheath and swiped it at the sword. It was knocked far enough away that Kane was able to use his other hand to push the man back with a forceful wind. The man flew back several feet and somersaulted, popping up to his feet. His sword fell to the ground and Kane wasted no time to go in for the final blows.

The man dove for his weapon, but Kane was quicker. He flicked his wrist, sending the sword skittering across the ground. Before his enemy could recover, Kane launched himself through the air and pulled the other dagger free of its sheath. The man lay on his back, looking up with wide eyes as Kane landed. His feet planted on either side of the man's body. He held his blades up menacingly, daring him to make a move.

"Yield," Kane said.

"I yield."

With those two little words, Kane was able to move on to the next round of the tournament. He helped the man to his feet as Ash and Quinn congratulated him on his victory, slapping him on the back. Kane felt exhilarated. He didn't want to leave this arena. Living without his powers was like torture. It was as if a part of his body was missing. He weaved his fingers in small signs before his face, sending the tiniest breeze through his hair.

Gabriel approached them. "Well done. Well done indeed, my boy. That man you just fought is nearly as old as I am. I'm quite surprised that you defeated him so quickly. If the rest of you are like your friend here, then we are in for an exciting day of fighting."

"Thank you, King Gabriel," Kane responded. "That was the most fun I've had in quite some time. I would say that guy had me worried for a minute, but I do my best not to tell lies."

The King chuckled, "Your friend here is a cocky one isn't he?"

Ash just laughed while Quinn said, "Sir, you don't know the half of it." Which just produced more laughs from them.

As King Gabriel was leaving, Kane's opponent approached them and asked, "What's your name, kid?"

"Kane. Yours" Kane asked, reaching out his hand.

"My name is Nereus. I'm very impressed by your skill. That wind magic you possess is nothing short of amazing."

Kane was pleasantly surprised to find that Nereus gripped his forearm in the customary handshake that Asmarians were accustomed to. *I guess we may have gotten that from Gabriel as well,* he thought.

"Thanks. I appreciate that. Honestly, I don't think I'd be much without my magic." Kane said, his eyes downcast.

Quinn said, "That's ridiculous, Kane. You're one of the strongest of our generation. You've helped Ash and I grow in, not only our abilities but our weapon handling as well."

"You think so?" He asked.

Ash chimed in, "Of course, man. I would bet good money that you could beat anyone here without your magic."

"I don't know about that." Nereus chuckled. "There are some *very* strong warriors here. I wouldn't even rank myself in the top ten. There's no need to be such a strong killer now that we've been down here for such a long time. But there are still men here who lived in the old days when our kingdom was above ground. They remember what it was like to take another's life. So be careful."

"I know we don't look like much," Ash said, "but the three of us have been through more battle than most others. We've had to kill to protect our homes and loved ones. Don't underestimate us."

"I didn't mean any disrespect. I just wanted to do my due diligence in offering you kids a proper warning. Good luck to you in the rest of your matches." And then the man left. Kane hoped they hadn't upset him; the last thing he wanted was to make actual enemies while they were stuck in the underground kingdom.

The Girl With The Atlantean Tattoo

"Next up will be Ash and Thaoc!" The announcer shouted.

Ash circled the giant that was standing in front of him. He wasn't sure why, but he hadn't felt like picking up a bow this time. He held a double-edged short sword in his hand and the giant had a hammer that was so large it would fit only in his hands. His arms were bigger than Ash's legs and his leg muscles were even larger. He wore a pair of brown shorts and leather-looking sandals. The rest of his body was free of armor or clothing of any kind. Ash could see old scars on his ripped chest. This man had a menacing look in his eyes.

Thaoc allowed Ash to get behind him. Ash smirked as he charged with his sword at the ready. Just before he was about to strike, the giant kicked his right leg back which landed directly to Ash's chest. He was sent flying backward several feet where he sprawled onto his back, his sword left in the dirt too far away to reach. His opponent was on him before he could recover. His giant hammer raised so high over his head that Ash knew he'd be obliterated if it made contact with him. In that split second, Ash wondered how safe this could be, what with the deadly weapons and all.

Before the hammer came crashing down, Ash hooked around the giant's ankle with his right arm. He thrust his hips up, his legs entangled around the giant's leg and clamping to the man's upper thigh with his knees pinched together. As he arched his back, his opponent fell over to the ground. Ash's grappling training had paid off. He scrambled to his feet and was faster than the giant. He dashed forward and threw a kick at his head.

The giant caught him with one hand, smirked, and then flung him farther than any human should be able to fling another. Ash had the wind knocked out of him on impact and stars dotted his vision. He needed to get some distance. *What was I thinking, trying to use a sword against this guy?*

Thaoc stood back so that Ash could stand. The head of his hammer rested on the ground, its handle leaned up against his hip. He had an amused smile splayed on his lips.

That's it, he thought. Ash had been holding back on using his magic, trying to even the battlefield. No more of that. Ash closed his eyes and removed the floodgates that were holding back the magical energy. It rippled down his body, flooding every inch of him. When he opened his eyes, they were glowing purple, and the smile on his opponent vanished.

Conjuring the lighting into his hands, he thrust his palms toward Thaoc, amethyst lighting zipped between them. With surprising speed, Thaoc raised his hammer, catching the brunt of the attack. No, his hammer was absorbing the lightning. Runes that Ash hadn't previously noticed were now glowing with a shade of mauve.

Ash cut off the lightning and stared at the man in disbelief. All he could get out was, "What the?"

Thaoc then swung his hammer horizontally in the air in

front of him with a roar. A blast of lightning erupted from it and Ash was frozen by the shock. His attack had been absorbed and then thrust back onto him, sending him into the dirt. The lightning didn't electrocute him like it would most people, it was more like an invisible force pushing him down, similar to how Kane's wind felt.

Thaoc was on him before Ash could recover. The giant head of the hammer was an inch from his face. The top had a blunt knob poised just before his eye. "Yield," the giant grumbled.

Breathing heavily, "I yield," he said.

Thaoc smiled and held out his massive hand. Ash took it and the giant pulled him to his feet. "That was fun. We should do that again sometime." Thaoc told him.

"Fun?" Ash chuckled, "You almost killed me!"

"I would do nothing of the sort!"

Ash had to know more about that hammer. "Man, how did you do that just now? That hammer just sucked my lightning right out of the air."

He beamed at his hammer, "This a legendary hammer of my people. Passed down for generations. It has seen more battle than any other weapon in our arsenal. It's called the Hammer of Ogun. It is said that the god Ogun, forged this hammer for mortals as a thank-you for their many years of worship. It can absorb most magical attacks, as well as other things."

"That's amazing," Ash said. "If you find one my size, let me know."

The man laughed, "I will certainly do that."

Up next was Quinn's first match. She was fighting a rather large man as well, however, this one wasn't nearly as big as Thaoc. Ash watched him try to hit her with a spear throw which she simply swatted aside with a wave of water. He leaned over and whispered to Kane, "Well that was dumb. Now he has nothing to fight with."

"It wouldn't have mattered," Kane said. "He lost the moment he faced her. She's just too good."

Kane was right. The man tried charging Quinn and she sent him careening to the ground by swiping his legs out from under him with water. She was conjuring the water quicker than he could take a breath. It was the quickest match thus far after Quinn wrapped an arm of liquid around his neck and he yielded.

"That was fast," Kane said.

They congratulated Quinn on her win as she advanced to the next round. Round two was starting and Kane was back up. This time he'd be fighting Thaoc. Ash was confident he'd be able to pull out the win, but he'd have to come up with a plan that would separate the giant from his hammer.

They traded attack attempts several times. Neither of them had been successful in landing a decent blow. Then Thaoc slammed the top of his hammer into Kane's abdomen. Ash winced from where he was watching. Kane crumpled over, heaving deep breaths as Thaoc went for the finished blow.

Kane swiped his hand horizontally, causing a wind to sweep the giant's feet out from under him. Kane lunged for the man as he drew a dagger from its sheath. He slashed the man's wrists one after the other. The hammer dropped to the ground, Thaoc's hands suddenly useless. He tried to get up, but Kane just knocked him back down with wind.

Wind began swirling around the hammer. It lifted into the air and started swinging. Even from this distance, Ash could hear the sound of the massive weapon cutting through the air. "Yield!" Kane yelled as he forced the wind to carry the swinging hammer closer to Thaoc. He was straining under the weight of the hammer, but Ash knew he had already won.

Thaoc held up his limp hands. "Okay. I Yield!"

Kane dropped the hammer back to the ground and slumped to his knees, clearly exhausted from the bout. A shaman walked over to Thaoc who held out his hands. The shaman held his wrists and muttered an incantation that Ash could only guess was the Atlantean language. Steam issued from the wounds as they closed up.

Quinn was up next for her second match of the day. The announcer called out, "Up next will be Quinn versus Kailani."

Ash and Kane looked at each other. "Another girl?" Ash asked as a tiny girl walked out onto the battlefield.

"It would seem so."

Ash caught Gabriel moving down from his seat to the ground where the competitors were. He sat next to the last guy Quinn fought. He was leaning forward with his elbows on his knees, his fingers laced in front of his face. He looked, was that worry on his face?

The tiny woman facing Quinn was covered in armor that gleamed. The flaming torches' light bounced off the golden plates. She had a helmet with her hair pinned up inside it tightly. Ash couldn't make out her features very well, but he could see that she had the same skin tone as the other Atlanteans. Runic symbols tattooed with white ink on her arms. She had a small, golden disc strapped to her waist. The center of the disk had been cut out except for a curved handle. Ash had no clue what the contraption was.

The mystery was answered soon enough. The fight began and the woman called Kailani drew the disc from its holster. She immediately flung it at Quinn who ducked. The disc flew over her head and then Kailani flexed her fingers. The disc came flying back, but Quinn didn't see it this time. The edge of the blade grazed her arm, leaving a shallow cut. Kailani caught the disc by the handle as she charged Quinn.

Recovering from the confusion of the disc attack, Quinn backed up, putting more distance between them. She conjured a wave of water and tried to entrap her opponent in a sphere. Kailani moved through the water as if it was just normal air. It didn't slow her down enough for Quinn to form another attack. Ash watched as the distance between them disappeared.

Kailani closed the space between herself and Quinn. She slid on the ground, entangling her legs with Quinns, and sweeping her with a scissor motion. She gained the top position, holding the edge of the disc to Quinn's neck, "Yield." She said.

"I yield. You win" Quinn lost the fight and, just as with Thaoc, a shaman ushered out to heal her wounds.

Ash hadn't realized how out of control his emotions were becoming. At some point within the last minute, his hair had begun to rise as the static in his body amplified. He hadn't noticed how tightly his fists were clenched until he released them, and the color returned to his white knuckles. He took a few deep breaths to calm down.

He didn't like seeing Quinn get hurt. It took all of his self-control to not run to her side even though he knew this was a friendly tournament. It didn't matter. His hands were trembling slightly when she took a seat next to him.

"Well, that was… interesting." She said. When he didn't respond she looked at him. "Are you okay?"

"Yeah, yeah, I'm fine." He didn't want her to see how vulnerable he was when it came to her.

She put her hand on his, "You know, I can tell when you're

not being completely honest with me."

Her touch seemed to calm him down, ever so slightly. "I'm fine now. I was just… worried."

She smiled, "Worried about me? Why would you do a thing like that?"

He wanted to say it was because he cared about her more than anything else, but all he could muster was, "Because you're my friend." Her smile faded and she withdrew her hand without another word.

Ash cursed himself for being so dumb about this. He didn't understand why it was so hard for him to express his true feelings.

The final match was Kane versus Kailani. Ash was excited about this fight. After seeing what that woman did to Quinn, he knew she would give Kane a run for his money. However, he also knew that Kane was the strongest warrior of their generation. It would be very entertaining, that's for sure.

It started pretty much the same as the previous match, but Kane was prepared for that bladed disc of hers. Instead of dodging it, he swatted it away with the flick of his wrist. Wind pushed it away from him and yet it somehow was called back to Kailani's hand. She charged him just as she did against Quinn. Kane blasted her with a gust of wind, and she was flung back several feet. She couldn't fight through the wind as she did water.

Ash had a feeling that Kane wasn't even breaking a sweat. He let the girl recover; she holstered her disc and ran at him, throwing a series of punches and kicks to no avail. He blocked every single one. Ash saw it before she did. Kailani left herself open and Kane threw a devastating side kick to her stomach. She lurched backward and then doubled over in pain.

"Had enough yet?" He heard Kane ask.

Kailani didn't answer, instead, as Kane waltzed forward she swung backwards. The back of her hand struck Kane in the face and Ash saw him smile with bloodied teeth. He turned back and she swung again but he ducked under her arm and was behind her before she could stop him. He wrapped his arm around her throat, putting her in a chokehold.

"Just yield!" He shouted as she struggled to claw herself free of his hold.

Then the unthinkable happened. Ash took in a sharp breath and everyone around him audibly winced as Kailani pulled her fist high in the air, then she swung down and nailed him right between the legs. He immediately let go of his chokehold and fell to the ground. She pulled her disc out again, placing a foot on his chest, and shouted, "Yield!"

Kane writhed under her foot, his chest heaving with labored breaths. She must not have been putting much weight on him because when he twisted under her and kicked her leg that wasn't on him, she came tumbling down. Her recovery was quick; she did a backward roll, and her helmet fell off as she jumped back up to her feet.

Even from this distance, Ash could see that she was stunning. Her appearance left him in a state of shock. Her hair was silvery white, eerily similar to Kane's. The contrast of the silver hair against her bronze skin was electrifying. It tumbled over her shoulder in a single braid. Ash glanced at Quinn and then Kane; they were both staring with wide eyes and raised eyebrows.

Ash didn't know if Kailani could see the surprise on Kane's face or if her timing was just a coincidence. She wasted no time. It had only been a couple of seconds since her helmet fell to the ground and she was already pouncing on him. Kane did not react when her elbow came flying at his face. There was a sickening crunch that shook Ash from his stupor, and then his best friend crumpled to the arena floor.

Traitor

The Forbidden were all scattered throughout the world currently. The only beings in Fingal's Cave—which is located on the uninhabited Scottish island of Staffa—were Aros, Augustus, and Draven. Augustus and his henchman had just returned to the cave after retrieving the Stone of Ruin.

The creation of shadow dragons makes moving around different parts of the world incredibly easy, as well as the shadow teleportation that Aros possesses. The dark lord had used up the vast majority of his strength in getting the Forbidden off Asmaria, not to mention he'd nearly died while inhabiting the boy. His life force drained as Ash's did also. Augustus had suggested attacking the Great Tree far sooner, but he insisted that he needed Ash's body first.

Carrying all their supplies, especially the obelisk, was essential to their escape. They didn't want to leave a trace of their existence behind for the Asmarians to find. The more anonymity they retained, the better. Augustus was just ready for all of it to be over. He never thought he would have turned into this, but the promise that Lord Aros had given him was something that he could not let slip by.

"Thank you for your help, Draven. You may go back to

Oban." Augustus told the young apprentice.

Draven said nothing, but bowed to show respect and then hopped back in the boat that brought them here. With Aros so weak, his powers had dulled which is why the Forbidden had been ordered to spread out and lay low while he recovered. There was a smaller chance they would be found if they weren't all in the same area.

Even now, Aros crouched in a small dark crevice inside the cave. He hunkered down like a child as Augustus approached. The master could still kill Augustus if he wanted to, but it would take more effort than before. Augustus knew that and that was partially why he continued to serve him. He feared that if he abandoned Aros, then he would grow strong once again and hunt the man down. That and he still wanted the paradise that was promised to him.

Augustus knelt in front of the shadowy figure that now looked like a child. "My Lord," he said. "We found it. The Stone of Ruin is ours. All we need now is to place it in the obelisk and your full power will return." He stood and retrieved the stone from his pocket and reached out to place it in the triangular hole of the obelisk.

"No," Aros hissed, a tendril of darkness wrapping around the man's wrist. "You mustn't place the stone into the obelisk. Not yet."

"What do you mean, my Lord?"

Aros' eyes glowed a brighter yellow and Augustus knew his anger was increasing. "I must be returned to the state of power I was in before being reduced to this... pathetic being. Bring my followers here. Gather them all and I will show you the ritual that will restore me to my former glory. Only then will you place that stone upon the obelisk, and then my power will increase tenfold."

"Understood, Master." Augustus put the Stone of Ruin back in his pocket. He would set out immediately to retrieve all the Forbidden. He touched the obelisk, siphoning off a bit of its power, and then teleported to another island where he knew a Forbidden member was laying low. He passed on the message and continued to the next. It was a tedious task, but one that only he could be trusted to perform.

Draven had only pretended to leave. He was surprised that neither of his leaders had noticed his presence, but the boy was always stealthy. He never had any sort of normality in his childhood. From the age of 10, he had begun training in the ways of the Forbidden. He was taught how to fight, how to deceive, and how to crush enemies with no mercy.

Never was he taught things about compassion or love. Even from his parents, who were cold toward him. They had been killed in the battle at Birkwood Park. There was a small part of him that was angry and sad when they died. A small part of him wanted revenge. But then he realized that he was living among the enemy.

Shortly thereafter, Draven began working his way up the ranks. He began hurting more and more of his comrades so that Augustus would notice him. Having power was the only way to get noticed, so he constantly put those who had been his friends in the infirmary. The more damage he did, the better.

Augustus came to him with the prospect of being his second-in-command after they fled Asmaria. He graciously accepted. All of this was his plan so that he could get close enough to them and take down the Forbidden from the inside. The opportunity to do so had not presented itself as of yet.

Draven was powerless and had not a single clue as to how he

would defeat either of his leaders. That part he hadn't thought through. He was so focused on reaching the top that he never stopped to figure out what he would do once that goal was surpassed. Now he listened from above the cave opening, the Forbidden leaders' voices echoing off the cave walls. They were planning to gather everyone here for some sort of ritual. He couldn't tell what it was, but he knew he had to do everything in his power to stop it.

That meant he would have to do the one thing that only he would be insane enough to do. As one of the top-ranking Forbidden warriors, he would have to seek the help of Asmaria. He climbed back down to his boat and took off. First, he would need some gasoline and provisions for the journey there. He remembered the way back. One thing that he was confident about was his memory. Once a place, a sight, or a word had crossed into his vision, he never forgot it.

Draven would go to Asmaria and plead with them to listen to him. He would make them listen at any cost. Even if he had to surrender his life to show how serious he was. The apprentice made a promise to himself and those like him—kids who hated living this way—that he would be the one to defeat the leaders of the Forbidden.

Kane Loses a Fight?

Ash and Quinn sprinted to Kane where he lay immobile on the arena floor. Ash could feel the anger prickling his skin. That familiar rage threatened to explode yet again. He felt the hairs on his arms begin to rise. He took a few deep, calming breaths and focused on helping his friend, but what could he do? The shaman was holding Kane's head in his hands muttering an incantation.

A faint green glow emanated from his palms, and within a few seconds, Kane's eyes fluttered open. Ash let out a sigh of relief. "What happened?" Kane asked.

Ash chuckled, "You got your butt handed to you by Kailani."

Kailani—who was by King Gabriel's side once again—had removed her armor, revealing a sky-blue tunic and matching pants. They approached as Kane regained his composure. Ash found Kane staring, seemingly entranced by the beauty of this woman. Gabriel stood in the center of the Atlanteum and spoke to the crowd with his booming voice.

"Good fights today. I hope that you all were entertained for a bit." The crowd of people cheered. "It is my pleasure to congratulate our winner Kailani, my very own daughter, and heir to the throne!" The cheers intensified.

She walked forward as Ash and the others gawked in silent exasperation. Ash never would have guessed that the massive, god-like figure of Gabriel could take part in creating someone so small and dainty-looking. She was a good fighter, no doubt about it, but from analyzing her fights, Ash could guess that she wasn't blessed with super speed or strength.

Gabriel embraced his daughter and had a proud smile when they broke apart. The two of them rejoined the three kids. "So, you're the King's daughter." Quinn said, matter-of-factly, "Do we call you princess?"

"Please," she said, sounding just short of indignant, "call me anything except that." That warranted a chuckle from the group.

The King said, "Yes, *Princess* Kailani," which made her scoff and roll her eyes, "hasn't quite taken to royalty as I originally hoped she would. Her life hasn't been the easiest though, so I tend not to fret too much. She'll grow into a great Queen in her own time."

"Father, please." Her eyes were pleading for him to stop talking.

"It's okay, my dear. Nothing that has happened to you is your fault." Gabriel tried to reassure her, but she stomped off anyway. When she disappeared, Kane shook his head like he was trying to clear a fog from his brain.

Gabriel continued, "She doesn't like to talk about it, but Kailani's mother died giving birth to her. We Atlanteans almost always develop great strength or speed as well, but she never did. She has other talents that set her apart, but instead of seeing it as a gift, she feels that it makes her an outcast. In her earlier years, she would try to make friends with the other children, but they avoided her. Now, she's not as friendly as I would like her to be."

"Sounds like she'd fit right in with us," Ash said, Quinn giving him a weird look. Was that jealousy in her eyes that he detected?

"I have to admit," Kane said, "that was a lot of fun. Do you mind if I get rid of some more energy before we leave?"

"No, no. Take all the time you need. I'll be back at the spell lab. Just meet me there when you're finished." The King took off and Ash hoped he left a chariot behind. Kane began propelling himself through the air with winds. Ash took note of the others in the crowd egressing from the arena.

When he was out of earshot, Quinn asked, "That Kailani is pretty, huh?"

He began to panic. Was this some sort of girl trap? "Um. Sure. I guess." *That* was not the answer Quinn wanted. She crossed her arms and walked away in a hurry. Ash thought to chase after her, but even if she stopped to listen, he had no idea what he would say. Kane floated back down and landed next to Ash softly.

"What's with her?" He asked.

"Girls are confusing, man." Ash knew Kane wasn't dating anyone, so he wasn't sure if he was the correct choice in asking for advice.

"Oh, I know it, brother. I once dated a girl who would get mad at me for training too much or hanging out with people who weren't her. She was crazy."

Ash chuckled, "I never knew you dated anyone." They began walking back through the arena, and upon exiting, Ash realized there was no chariot waiting. They would have to trek back to the center of the city.

When Ash and Kane returned to the spell lab, Quinn was

already there with Gabriel. As they approached, the King said, "Unfortunately, it's not ready. I have many rooms in my palace that you can choose from. You'll have to stay until the elixir is complete."

That wasn't the news Ash wanted, but he wasn't upset over it. He was about to live in the palace of Atlantis which he thought was cool, even if it was temporary. The King took them back to the palace and led them up the stairs and to the door positioned behind the throne. They climbed up the spiral staircase, flaming torches flickering as they brushed by.

The door they entered was a long hallway with a burgundy carpet. Torches and paintings filled both walls. Gabriel showed them which rooms were empty and the one Ash chose was huge on the inside. He'd never seen a bed so big, a tub so deep, or ceilings so high. There was an armoire that he found had a plethora of Atlantean clothing.

After soaking in the swimming pool-sized bath for ages, he tried on different outfits. He went through several different combinations of clothing, trying on everything from swimwear to battle attire. There was a plethora of armor to choose from. There was a mail coif that he tried on which made him feel like he was being pressed down by gravity. He tried on plate armor and leather armor, then found a rustic, teal helmet that felt like it weighed fifty pounds.

Then Ash found something worth keeping; it was a long night shirt that had been tucked away in the bottom of the armoire. It was a similar shade of purple as the shirt that he always wore, except this one had sparkling silver specks woven into the material. He slipped it on and was momentarily whisked away by a cloud. It was the softest material he'd ever laid on his skin.

I never want to take this off, he thought. Ash wondered if the King would allow him to keep the nightshirt as a parting gift, they were just pajamas after all. He would ask him the next chance he got. Now though, he was exhausted. The battles from the day had made him weary.

Before turning in, Ash walked over to the tall double doors and heaved them open. He stepped out onto the balcony and took in the sight before him. He could see the whole city on this side of the palace. In the distance, the bioluminescent creatures crawled around on the walls at a snail's pace. How interesting that this far down it was nothing but solid rock when thousands of years ago this kingdom was floating on the ocean. He imagined the glowing creatures were stars, and could see how beautiful it must have been to stand out here in the dead of night.

A Fast Trip Home

Quinn had long since lost track of time down in the city of Atlantis. She tried to calculate how many normal days had gone by since they dropped in, but it was no use. Time was—as they say—different here. The elixir for the Tree still wasn't complete and she was beginning to worry that they would return home to nothing. The Forbidden had warned that the Great Tree would die, and our island would be plunged into the ocean.

She didn't want to believe that, but she was beginning to have doubts. Based on the number of times they had gone to bed—which wasn't the only factor she needed, seeing as it could be the middle of the day above ground when they nap—it felt like weeks had passed by. They would train with all their spare time, practicing different fighting techniques that the Atlantean warriors showed them, or just having more battles in the Atlanteum.

Quinn noticed that Kane would always gravitate toward Kailani whenever he got the chance. She was one of the most beautiful beings that Quinn had ever laid eyes on, and admitting that to herself just hurt her confidence and self-esteem. She knew what Ash would say when she asked if he thought Kailani was pretty. And yet, his answer still hurt her deeply. It was jealousy. She knew that but was unable to prevent it from occurring. She wasn't sure why she even asked such a silly question.

She and Ash had many moments together over the past several months. He and Rick had celebrated her fourteenth birthday with her family. They'd trained together almost every day. A lot of it involved grappling, which often left Quinn with a knot of nervousness in her stomach. She kept waiting for Ash to say something, to ask her to be his girlfriend, or to just tell her that he had feelings for her if that was even the case. However, it still hadn't happened. She was trying to be patient, but her patience was wearing thin.

There was another friendly tournament scheduled for today and Quinn had grown tired of them. The outcome was always the same. If Kailani competed, she won. If she didn't compete, Kane won. Every time they faced each other, she would let down her braided hair, and Kane would stand there like a buffoon. *Boys are dumb,* she would think every time Kane would get knocked out because he couldn't take his eyes off the girl.

Quinn caught Ash sneaking back to his room one night. He was wearing a long shirt that hung down to his knees. He had an armful of bread that he'd swiped from the kitchen. She imagined he would be embarrassed if he knew she had seen him.

It seemed like every day he was growing more muscular and getting better at fighting. She was no longer able to beat him in their sparring matches, with or without magic. She was happy for it though. She knew he would be vital in the war against the Forbidden. Quinn also admired him for not taking it easy on her like some guys would.

Another day of battles was just beginning in the Atlanteum. The announcer was calling out the first round; it was Kane versus Ash. The fight began, but before any strikes could be made, Quinn saw a little boy run up to Gabriel and whisper something in his ear. He stood up and shouted, "Stop!"

Gabriel walked briskly toward them, and Quinn joined them in the arena. "The elixir is ready," Gabriel told them. "I assumed you would want to leave immediately."

Kane looked between the others who nodded to him, "Yes sir. We need to get back home."

"You know, your strength would be unrivaled in the war against Aros," Kane said to Gabriel. They were gathered in front of the palace. Kane had told them their dragons would have returned home by now. They would have no way to get back, but the King assured them he had just the thing. "I know you've already done more than enough for us, but if you're itching for some action, our Guardians wouldn't turn you away."

Gabriel handed Kane the elixir which was a bright green color. He looked like he was considering the possibility, but then said, "I must admit, I do miss real battle, as brutal as it is. You never feel as alive as you do while so close to death. However, I must run this kingdom. If I leave, Atlantis will be without a ruler. My daughter isn't ready for that level of responsibility." Kane glanced at Kailani, whose eyebrows were knit together in frustration.

"Now," the King said, "I have a few more gifts for each of you. I refuse to part ways without doing my best to make you stronger warriors. These should help." The elders who had interrogated them emerged from the gathered crowd. They carried several items in their arms. They sat a long box on the ground and opened it, revealing a magnificent-looking bow. The recurve of the bow was a dark blue. The string nocks were white and the string itself was black.

One of the elders picked it up and held it out to Ash, "Go ahead. Give it a try."

"But I don't have any arrows."

"You won't need any," the old man said.

Ash looked as confused as Kane felt, but he did what the elder said. He picked it up and smiled, purple lightning crackled to life around the surface of the bow. "I can feel the power coming off this thing." Ash pulled the string back, aiming at the ground just a few feet away. An arrow made of pure lightning magic manifested and he released it. The arrow erupted in a shower of sparks as it connected.

"How did you do that?" Quinn asked him, but he just shrugged.

The old man explained, "That bow is called Beithir. You will not need arrows for it, however, it will shoot normal arrows just fine. It will also never break. And its final feature is that you need not carry it all the time. Allow me." He retrieved the bow from Ash and turned his wrist over so that his palm was facing up. He slapped his wrist with the bow, and he winced as the bow vanished before their eyes.

"Where'd it go?" Ash asked.

"Look here." The elder pointed to Ash's wrist and a tiny, white tattoo of a bow had appeared. "Now then to retrieve it, all you have to do is hold out your hand and imagine that you are recalling the bow from wherever it may be."

Ash did as the man said, and this time the bow snapped back into his hand with a faint cracking noise. "Wow," Ash said. "I don't know what to say. I guess all I *can* say is thank you. I'm very grateful for the hospitality you all have shown us." He bowed to them and stepped back.

"As for you," one of the elder women said, approaching Quinn. "We have something a little more… permanent in mind. With your blessing, of course."

"Uh, sure," Quinn said. "Go ahead."

The elder covered Quinn's forearm with her hand and muttered something in Atlantean. A blue glow emanated from beneath her palm and Quinn's skin sizzled, causing her to grimace as something was being burned into her flesh. When it was done, Kane and Ash both looked over her shoulder to see what had been done to her. Near the bend of her elbow was a small, blue, diamond-shaped symbol. Inside the diamond was a series of snowflake shapes. Kane found it quite pretty, however, he had no idea what it meant.

"This is the mark of Cailleach," the elder explained. "When you breach our wards, and your power returns you will find out what it does. I can tell you that it will greatly enhance your abilities, however, there is no way to know for sure the effect it will have."

Quinn bowed and said, "Thank you."

"And now you." Another elder motioned for Kane to come closer. "You too will have to wait until your power returns to figure out what this does. Here, give me your hands."

Kane held his hands out and the man placed a golden ring on each thumb. He felt a hum of energy from them, and white runes glowed as they made contact with his skin before fading. "The rings of Sidhe. Very powerful artifacts."

"Thank you," he said with a bow. Then the three were ushered into a small circle drawn in the dirt.

King Gabriel said, "Since I know where Asmaria is I will be the one to cast this spell. It should be fine, but just to be safe you should all think about your home when I do this. It's been an honor to aid you in this war. Perhaps our paths will cross again one day. If not in this life, then the next."

Kane heard every word, and those words meant a lot to him, but he couldn't react. He'd just laid eyes on Kailani again. He had grown accustomed to spending time with her over the last few weeks, or however long it had been since they arrived in Atlantis. They shared details about their lives with each other and sparred fairly often. She was a great fighter. The disc she carried is called a chakram. Kane had never seen anything like it, but Kailani told him that it was a birthday gift from her father. The disc was attuned to her energy, so she was able to recall it back to her hand after throwing or dropping it.

He decided that she was the most beautiful girl he'd ever seen, and after getting to know her a little better, he would stop his pursuit of being the strongest mage even if it meant he could be with her. His chance was vanishing now as the King chanted in Atlantean. She made eye contact with him and he almost stepped outside the circle. Almost. He cared too much about his home to throw it all away on a girl who probably didn't even feel the same way as he did. It was too hard; he closed his eyes.

Kane then felt the presence of another body that was very close to his. A body that wasn't there a moment before. When he opened his eyes, there was a head of braided, silvery hair. He looked down and their feet were beginning to glow a bright yellow. His legs felt weirdly fuzzy. The last thing he heard was the incantation of Gabriel ending and then Kailani saying something that sounded like, "kelob tem, tabe tow." And then everything vanished.

95

Prison Break

Avani volunteered to endure what he knew would be torture first. He'd partook in his fair share of dealing out pain to individuals with the information they needed, and now it was time to have that favor returned. The plan was to bust the three Guardians out of their prison cell as quietly as possible so that they could recover their strength in the shadows. Once they were strong enough, they would launch a full-scale attack on Ember and any of the others who stood in their way. It was a horrible realization to know that they would be attacking their own, however, they all agreed that it was necessary to protect Asmaria from its people.

Morsels of food and water were brought to them on what seemed like a weekly basis. The Guardians were feeling better, but the battle had only just begun. They wouldn't be able to do anything until their hands were free. From what they could tell, there was almost always one of Ember's guards outside so that made it difficult to sneak supplies to them. They would have to wait for whichever guard standing there at the time went for a bathroom break.

It took the others a long time to come to check on the—now four—residents of this particular cell. A small hammer and chisel had been slipped to Rick so that he could chip away at the concrete covering their hands. That and small pieces of leather for them to bite down on; the guards were usually far enough away that they wouldn't hear the chipping of the concrete, however, tortured screams would be a different story.

Avani had no pain for a while. The hammer and chisel pinging against the concrete, breaking it apart, bit by tiny bit. And then as the block wore down he began to feel it. He was already holding the leather between his teeth, but now he had to bite down. The man was no stranger to pain and it wasn't unbearable yet. He could feel the concrete pulling at his chafed skin, causing him to grimace.

"You okay?" Rick asked. Avani nodded his head.

Rick continued chipping away. He would stop every few whacks to make sure Avani was doing okay and wanted to keep going. Avani almost told him to stop at one point, but realized if he stopped and started back later on it would just be worse the second time. Around an hour in the majority of the concrete had been knocked away. Avani had sweat rolling down his face and his breathing was labored, his chest rising and falling rapidly.

"I think we should take a break," Rick suggested.

Avani could feel his heart pounding but shook his head frantically, and tried to say, "No, keep going." It came out muffled but he assumed Rick understood well enough because he shook his head slightly and started hammering again. He wasn't sure how many, but Avani could tell that the bones in his hands and fingers were already broken. It was almost too much to handle. At one point he closed his eyes and wasn't sure if he had blacked out or not, but then Rick said, "I think that's all we're gonna get for now."

Avani opened his eyes and looked down; his hands were mostly free. There were still pieces of concrete stuck to his skin, and the visible skin was nothing but a bloody mess. His hands were swelling from the broken bones, and he could his pulse throbbing in them. His mouth opened and the leather dropped, saliva strung down his chin, and he breathed heavily. He tried to flex his fingers but the tiniest movement sent stabbing pain throughout his hands, causing him to wince.

"You ladies sure you want to do this?" Rick asked the other two.

Avani heard Leena scoff, "Don't insult us. We're just as tough as Avani, whether he wants to admit it or not." Even with his hands throbbing, that made him laugh.

The next couple of hours were almost worse than getting his hands hammered on and broken. He had to listen to each of his fellow Guardians fight to stay quiet through the torture. The pings of the hammer weren't the only thing echoing in their cell. He had to listen to their pained groans with each smack. Leena went after Avani and when her hands were free they looked almost identical to his. Bora went last and she looked rough, but her hands didn't look as bad as theirs. She must have had a little wiggle room in her encasing.

Tears were drying on Bora's face as she asked, "What's next?"

Rick thought for a moment then said, "Well, considering I doubt any of you can wield magic right now." He paused as if it were a question, looking between the three of them. They each shook their heads. "We'll have to wait for the others to come back. With the guards always being nearby, there's no telling when the next time they'll come by will be, but hopefully, it's soon."

The prison cell opened and the Guardians were quickly

ushered out. Avani could taste the freedom on his lips. He saw some familiar faces amongst those helping them escape. They scurried through the city streets and into the jungle. They slowed to a walk once they entered the concealment of the trees. They walked to an outpost on the edge of the island where a couple of the water mages were positioned, working the currents of the ocean to prevent anyone from getting close.

Avani was unsure of whose side they were on, and if they were on the wrong side, they would most likely attempt to raise the alarm. The mages with good hands stormed into the hut, demanding to know where their allegiance lies. It was not with them. They were knocked out cold before they knew what was happening.

"Okay," Rick said, "with that out of the way, you all can rest up here for a bit. We'll keep a lookout and run supplies to you whenever possible. Moving around the Capital will be much harder now. Especially for me. It's safe to say that I haven't garnered much trust since being here, and this certainly won't help."

"If it's any consolation," Bora said, "you've earned my trust. My life is indebted to you." And the others nodded.

He smiled, "I'm just trying to do the right thing here. And we need to be ready for when the kids come back."

That's right. It had been many weeks since the kids left on their mission to find that which would save the Great Tree. They could return at any moment and Avani wanted to be ready for when they did. He assumed that chaos would ensue as soon as they attempted to approach the Tree. He wasn't positive, but he was fairly certain that Ember would have the Tree guarded 24/7. That is precisely what he would done if he were on the other side of this predicament.

While the others were talking amongst themselves and Avani was lost in thought, no one heard or saw the boat motor on its way to the shoreline. It wasn't until the door to the hut opened did any of them realize they weren't alone. Avani whirled around, the movement of his hands causing him to wince and take in a sharp breath. The other four mages jumped in front of the Guardians and Rick, their hands ready to wield. The young man standing in the doorway was a silhouette against the moonlight shining behind him. His face was downcast and the hood of his black cloak—the same that the Forbidden wear—was draped over his head.

"State your business here or die where you stand," Carter, a fire mage said with his hands emblazoned.

The man turned his face upward and Avani was surprised to see the visage of a young man. He looked to be just a couple of years older than Kane. He held his hands up in a brief surrender and then reached for the hood, pulling it back off his head.

"My name is Draven and I have information about the Forbidden that you'll *definitely* want."

A Close Call

Kane's vision and body reappeared simultaneously. He looked around and saw that they all had made it except for Ash. Where was he? Kane had no clue what could have caused him to be sent somewhere else. The sun was peaking over the horizon, casting brilliant orange and pink across the morning sky. Kane noticed that they were only a couple hundred meters from the Great Tree. Soon they would save it and restore the Tree's health. Then he saw the silvery hair a few feet away and remembered that Kailani had joined them at the last second.

"Kailani," he said, "why did you do that? You'll never be able to return home now!"

She had a guilty look in her eyes when she said, "I was never meant to be Queen of Atlantis. Father wouldn't listen; I told him I didn't want to be a ruler, but he would never listen. I couldn't take another second of living underground. I'd only seen paintings of how the rest of the world looked. From what I've seen in books, they don't do it justice. The sky… it's beautiful." She peered up at the sky with awe in her eyes.

"What about your father?" Quinn asked.

"My father will be okay. I asked him to forgive me. It may

take some time, but he'll get over it eventually."

So that's what she had said to him. "Where's Ash?" Quinn asked, looking around frantically. Her breath labored and panic was written across her face.

"Just try to calm down," Kane said. "We'll find him later. Right now we have to save the Tree. Let's go." They took off at a brisk jog toward the Tree. The sun was creeping higher, casting shadows all over the place. Kane looked around vigilantly as they approached. Something felt off, but he didn't know what it was. Just as they were roughly twenty feet away from the Tree, the ground beneath his feet swirled up to his knees, locking him tightly into place. Kane looked around and the others were in the same trap.

Mages began filtering in around them from where they were hiding and he heard one of them issue the order for Ember to be brought immediately. It would seem they were guarding the Great Tree to stop the kids when they returned. Kane didn't know if he would be fast enough to retrieve the elixir from his bag and hurl it at the tree from this distance and with him being surrounded by mages. If the vial were to shatter before reaching the Tree, they would all be doomed.

"Come on, guys. We're just trying to save the Tree. Let us go." Kane pleaded to the Guild members around them. Many of them he recognized and had trained with, but by the looks on some of their faces it would seem like they were strangers.

A burly fire mage named Will stepped forward, igniting a flame in his palm, "You make any sort of move toward the Tree and I'll melt you where you stand."

Kane scoffed and rolled his eyes. He was annoyed that they *actually* believed that he and the others were trying to make the Tree worse. The sun was shining enough light for him to get a good look at it. The Great Tree was worse. Its bark was mostly black now. 99% of its leaves had fallen to the ground and it looked like it was going to be done for any second now. They had to get the elixir to it!

"Well, if you aren't a sight for sore eyes." Kane heard the familiar voice of Ember as the man walked up from behind them. "And here I thought you all had died while on your quest. Or maybe I just hoped for it."

"What is wrong with you?" Quinn asked. "Let us go, psychopath."

Kane could see the malice in the man's eyes, "Watch your tongue, little girl." His gaze flickered over to Kailani, "And who is this? My, you're a pretty one aren't you?" Kane felt a ripple of anger flash through his body. He could feel the power coursing through him. "Where is Ash?" Ember looked nervous as he turned to the other mages and ordered, "Find him! He's probably sneaking around here now!"

The Guild members scattered out and began searching for Ash, but Kane smirked as he knew they wouldn't find him. Now he might have a chance to save the Tree since Ember was the only one watching them. He slowly loosened his pack from his shoulders. The movement caused Ember to snap his attention back to the boy. His eyes glowed orange as flames flickered around his fingers.

"What are you doing? What's the plan? Come back here and finish the Great Tree off for good?"

Kane shook his head in exasperation, "Would you listen to yourself? Just look at the Tree! It's going to croak any second now! Why would we need to finish it off? It would make more sense to just wait it out."

Ember seemed to consider it for a moment but, then said, "I

will not be made a fool by traitorous scum like you. You can join your other Guardians in their grave."

Fear and worry hit Kane like a punch to the face, "What did you do to them?" He shouted.

Ember chuckled, "Don't worry. They're probably still alive. However, I doubt for much longer. Then it will be just me to rule Asmaria. I will have successfully rid them and all of you from this island while the Guild believes it was all their choice. It's priceless!"

Kane had become increasingly dismayed. Quinn seemed to corroborate that feeling as she shouted, "There won't be an island if you don't save the Tree, moron!"

The insult must have upset the Guardian because he turned on her, his flames building intensity. He stomped toward her. Kane couldn't let him hurt his friend. What did he have that he could use? He reached for a karambit; it would be harder to throw than the usual weapons he was used to throwing, but he could probably control it with wind magic. He'd have to try anyway.

A flash of movement on the other side of Quinn caught Kane's attention. Kailani's hand was outstretched and the chakram had flown past Ember, grazing his shoulder. He winced and clutched the wound, cauterizing it immediately. He then thrust his hand toward her with a growl, spitting flame out which hurled toward her face.

"No!" Kane yelled and sent a gust of wind in their direction. The flames directed at Kailani were pushed to the side. Ember stumbled slightly from the force of the wind. Kane had to get out of this dirt. He began clawing at the earthen prison, but it seemed like it was made mostly of rock. He looked over at Kailani and her eyes were wide with fear. Quinn had her hands behind her and they made eye contact. She nodded to her hands and he saw that she was funneling small amounts of water into the ground to soften its hold on her. With luck, she would be able to escape and take out Ember.

The man recovered and Kane could see anger in the man's eyes. "You'll pay for that. I'm going to make sure you suffer. I was going to make your death quick, but now I think I'll do things a little differently. First, I'm going to kill your little friends here and make you watch. Then, I'm going to drag your parents out here in front of you and kill them as well. Only then, after you've suffered through watching everyone you love die, then I will grant you the mercy of death."

Time was up. If Kane was going to save the Tree, it had to be now. He quickly grabbed his pack and reached inside to grab the vial of elixir. He felt its glassy surface against his fingertips and saw Ember begin to run towards him. Before he could yank it free, however, the ground then swallowed the three of them up to their necks. The pack laid a foot away from his face.

No! He thought. He tried to look around, but couldn't turn his head much. An earth mage walked around in front of them. "No worries, sir. They won't be doing anything now." More of the Guild was now returning to the area. "We searched all around the Tree in a wide arc. Ash is nowhere to be found."

A cunning smile spread across Ember's face, "I see. So, Ash didn't make it here did he? What, did he die on your journey? Did he get lost?"

Kane had a sense of hopelessness set in. "I don't know."

Ember laughed and others around them joined in. "Now then. Let's see what was so important inside this bag, shall we?"

Kane thought to protest, but what would be the point? They were purely at the mercy of this maniac. He could only hope that he would see reason in the end and pour the elixir on the Tree. Kane watched as Ember pulled the glowing green liquid free of his bag and held it up in the air to inspect it more thoroughly.

"You see?" He said. "They've come with another poison to finish off the tree." Murmurs spread throughout the gathered mages. "As the current one, and only, Guardian, I hereby sentence you three to death. I don't even know who you are," he pointed at Kailani, "but it's clear you are an accomplice. Perhaps you supplied them with this deadly swill. Is there any of you who oppose my ruling?"

Much to Kane's horror, not a single hand went up. Not a single mage stepped out from the crowd to defend him. He looked around as much as he could to try pleading, if only with his eyes, to those he recognized. Maybe it was his fault for never bothering to make many friends. Maybe he should have considered having more people on his side would help in a pinch. How could he have known his life would ever come to this though? He couldn't. He wouldn't blame himself for being too goal-oriented to focus on friendship. He did, however, promise to make the most of his time with his friends if they made it out of this alive.

"First things first," Ember announced. "We must rid the world of this." He held up the elixir. Kane and the other two protested with different shouts, but he ignored them. He lifted the vial high above his head and then another familiar voice rang out, "Stop!"

Ember froze with his hand lifted over his head. The ground loosened around the kids and they crawled free. He spun around to see Avani, Bora, and Leena approaching with a few others in their wake. "You have committed enough crimes already," Avani told Ember. "Are you kids okay?" He asked them.

"Better now." Kane breathed a sigh of relief. "That elixir will save the Tree. We have to get it to her now!"

"You heard him, Ember. Hand it over." Leena said, taking a step forward.

Ember chuckled, "I've come this far. You can't stop me now!" And then his hand dropped with great speed. Kane wasn't used to being the one frozen with fear of a situation. But now he found himself watching everything unfold. It was as if he was having an out-of-body experience and was able to see what was happening from different angles at the same time.

Kailani's hand thrust upward and the chakram came soaring back, zipping through the crowd of people, only nicking them as it passed. Quinn's hands shot out, conjuring a small wave of water. The tattoo that had been given to her by the Atlantean elders was glowing blue. The vial of potion left Ember's hand and was inches away from smashing to bits. The wave that Quinn conjured slid beneath the glass vial and swirled around it. With a quick clench of her fists, the water froze, keeping the vial safe behind a thick sheen of ice. As the ice solidified, the chakram embedded itself into the back of Ember.

The man's eyes went wide, and a line of crimson blood trickled from his mouth as he muttered, "How?" And then he fell to the ground. Everyone seemed to be in the same state of shock. Too surprised to say or do anything. Kane looked at Quinn and she looked just as surprised at her new ability as everyone else. She stared at her palms questioningly.

"It seems the Atlantean gifts are pretty wicked, huh?" Kane

asked her.

"Uh-huh," was all she could muster.

The reality of the situation kicked back in and Kane ran over to the wave of ice. "Any idea how to get the elixir out of there?"

"Let me try something," Quinn said. She held her hands out and strained against an invisible force. Nothing happened for a few seconds, but then the ice rapidly melted and returned to its original state. The vial flipped and twisted, suspended in the water. Kane reached in slowly, mesmerized by this new power Quinn had. He plucked the vial from the liquid as it splashed into the ground.

Kane jumped to his feet and proceeded toward the tree. A group of Guild members gathered together, blocking his way. They were still keen on keeping them away from the Tree. With the tiniest flick of his wrist, Kane was launched over their heads. As he floated over them, he glanced at the rings on his thumbs and noticed that the runes were glowing with a white hue.

A chunk of rock was hurled at him from one of the earth mages, threatening to crush him in the sky. With another flick of his wrist, Kane lurched to the side, narrowly avoiding the boulder. It would appear that the rings gifted to him allowed his ability to increase substantially. He could use wind magic with less effort.

Kane wasted no time as he landed next to the Tree. He didn't even bother uncorking the vial. He threw it from a few feet away, and blasting it with wind so that it would soar at an incredible speed. The glass shattered and the green liquid ran down the bark. It trickled down the black trunk until it hit a group of exposed roots. A shockwave issued from the Great Tree, knocking Kane to the ground. The Great Tree shuddered as the roots soaked up the potion. Kane sat back up and saw the black bark slowly turning back to its original color.

The last leaf fluttered to the ground as the black bark disappeared and simultaneously, new leaves started to sprout. By the time the branches were filled with new foliage Kane thought it looked even more magnificent than before. He turned around to see the awestruck faces of his fellow Guild members. They were on their knees staring up at the Great Tree. At that moment, the relief Kane was feeling was sucked out of his mind by the anger that replaced it.

He beckoned the wind to replace the ground beneath him and it listened. His body hovered above them while his fingers conjured the winds effortlessly. He stood on the wind and commanded the others to answer him, "You should all be ashamed of yourselves. What would you have done if we hadn't saved the Tree?" He waited for an answer but only got stunned looks from Ember's accomplices. "Answer me!" Kane bellowed.

The anger was feeding into the wind magic, whipping everyone's hair and clothes in every direction. He wanted to hurt them. Never before had he felt like this. And then someone touched his shoulder; he looked over to find Bora's face. She was weaving frantic signs with her hands to keep herself afloat next to him. "You've done well," she shouted over the whip of the wind. "But it's time to let us handle the Guild, okay?"

She was right and he knew it. He was still a teen, even though he'd done more for this world than the majority of the adults here. He nodded his head and returned to the ground. He wasn't yet a Guardian, and perhaps this outburst was a sign that he had much to learn about being leading people.

"Now then," Avani addressed the Guild, "A Guild meeting is to happen immediately. Spread the word to those who aren't here. Attendance will be taken and if you're not there, we will assume your absence as a dereliction of duty. There will be dire consequences. Now go." The group dispersed and disappeared into the jungle in the direction of the Capital. Avani walked over and held his arm out, Kane clasped his forearm and they gave the customary Asmarian shake to each other. "I'm proud of you. All of you." His eyebrows were knit as he noticed Kailani. "Where is Ash?"

Quinn shook her head and answered with a shudder, "We don't know. We all left at the same time but he didn't make it here." Kane could see how worried she was. He put his arm around her as a comfort.

"I'm sure he's fine, wherever he is," Kane said and then motioned for Kailani to join his side. "This is Kailani. She comes from Atlantis."

They greeted each other, exchanging introductions. Kane saw Avani go over and retrieve the disc from Ember's back and then check for a pulse. He seems he had passed because Avani used his earth magic to roll the man's body over to the Great Tree. He looked over his shoulder as the roots wrapped around him, "Let's hope giving him back to the Tree doesn't backfire in some way." He handed the disc back to Kailani who cleaned it off and returned it to its holster at her hip.

"Well," Leena said, "first order of business is to find out what to do with all of Ember's accomplices. After that, we can begin looking for Ash."

"There are more pressing matters than whoever this Ash kid is," one of the people behind them growled. Kane hadn't noticed him until he spoke, and now that he looked, realized that he didn't recognize him but something about him was off-putting.

"Who are you?" Kane asked, stepping forward with his hand behind his back, already gripping a karambit.

"I'm the guy trying to save everyone," he muttered. Kane narrowed his eyes. What was he talking about? Who was he? He couldn't have been much older than Kane. He looked young. Then Kane noticed why he looked odd. He wasn't wearing mage clothes. Kane ripped the karambit free of its sheath.

"You're with the Forbidden," Kane growled.

Avani held up a hand, "Just hold on, Kane. We can explain. He's here to help." Kane elected to trust his Guardians and sheathed his weapon.

"Fine, but you better not say another word about Ash or—" his threat was interrupted by the loudest crack of lightning and thunder he'd ever heard. They all ducked down and spun toward the direction of the sound. A massive figure had appeared in the sky. It looked to be a bird of some sort.

"To the Capital, hurry!" Avani demanded. They all took off, running as quickly as possible to gather the other mages for this new threat.

Kane wasn't sure what the thing was, maybe it was some sort of wicked beast sent by the Forbidden. Maybe it was something entirely different. Whatever the thing was, he didn't want to fight it right now. Normally, he wouldn't shy away from a battle, but right now he was feeling weary.

Lost and Found

"Think about your home." That's what Gabriel had said. So then why was Ash standing outside on a city street that looked nothing like Asmaria? *Wait, am I back in New York?* He asked himself. Zero time had seemingly passed between his body disappearing, the whoosh that filled his ears along with total darkness, and then reappearing on this sidewalk. The building in front of him looked like the old apartment building he and Rick lived in. What went wrong?

"Did I think of this place when he told us to think of our home?" Ash was talking to himself now. He tried to remember, but for some reason, the image he'd previously thought of had fled his mind and he could no longer recall which home he'd pictured. After the confusion faded, the anger settled in. He took some deep, calming breaths and tried to formulate a plan. He had trained for every sort of situation over the past few months. He told himself that this wasn't a big deal. Walking, away from the building, he tried to clear his mind but his thoughts were interrupted.

"Hey kid," a man from behind him said. "Can you spare some change?" Ash turned around to see two rather large men standing there with sly smirks on their faces. They looked like predators who'd just found their next meal. Something was off about them. Ash realized what it was; the black clothing they were wearing.

Ash's body began to hum with energy. He was so elated to have it back. They began to saunter forward slowly, menacingly. Ash reached out his hand and with a snap, his bow Beithir was in his hands. He had a lightning arrow nocked before the two Forbidden goons had time to process what just happened. "I wouldn't take another step forward if I were you."

The men didn't care to listen. After their surprise faded, Ash saw that same devilish look enter their faces once again. They spread out a bit and the shadows around started to swell and curl in toward Ash. Then they flickered and vanished. One of the men cursed, "Ugh, why did Aros have to be so weak?"

Ash didn't waste any more time. He loosed the arrow at the man on the right and had another arrow ready before the man's body hit the ground. The second guy's eyes widened and he turned to run, but Ash shot him through the back before he could get far. He too, crumpled to the ground. Ash looked around, hoping no one had seen him. The last thing he needed was to be arrested for murder here.

What were they doing here? He wondered. *Aros is weak? Good. That'll make it easier to destroy him.*

Then Ash remembered something else. He saw Kailani jump into their circle and mutter some words in Atlantean. He wondered where she'd gone. How could it be that she made it to Asmaria if that is in fact where she wound up? It just seemed unfair that Ash was sent here.

Ash needed to find a way home, fast. But how? There weren't exactly any airlines he could pay to take him to Asmaria. Perhaps he could find a boat to rent, but how would he know which direction to go, and how would he pay for it?

Ash was so incredibly frustrated with his situation. He walked around aimlessly, unsure of how much time had gone by since he'd landed in New York. There were a few moments when he felt a tugging sensation in his gut but ignored it each time. *Just look where my intuition has gotten me so far.* He kept looking for a place to rent a boat, deciding that he'd figure out how to pay the boat captain at a later time.

It seemed apparent that this tugging sensation wasn't going to leave him alone. After convincing a particularly well-dressed man to give up his freshly purchased hotdog, Ash scarfed it down, savoring the old taste of home that he'd not experienced in a long time. The tug pulled him away from the direction he was previously planning to follow. Ash's luck began to turn as soon as he made the conscious decision to have his feet follow his gut.

He tripped. Ash stepped off a curb to cross the street and his foot slipped on a candy wrapper. He slammed into the ground, scraping the palms of his hands. *It's okay,* he thought, *I've had worse days.* Ash was trying to remain calm and continue. Then a car almost hit him. The yellow cab was only a few inches from smacking into him.

His frustration was steadily increasing. It's like his luck had suddenly shifted and now the whole city was trying to hurt him or thwart his progress in getting back to Asmaria. First, it was tripping and then it was the car. After that, a pigeon pooped on his head and he had to find a public bathroom to clean his hair up. Then he stepped in a mud hole that soiled his pant leg halfway between his ankle and knee.

He ended up finding himself approaching a small forest and decided to blow off a little steam. The magical energy had been prickling his skin with each unfortunate event that happened to him. His fingertips were already beginning to spark so he took off at a sprint into the woods. He found a massive boulder and decided it was the perfect target. He began sending lightning bolts into it. The lightning wasn't intense enough to melt the rock, however, with each arc of electricity, the rock glowed a brighter orange.

After Ash felt like he had burned off enough of the steam, he retreated from the woods and continued walking, giving in to that annoying pull. Eventually, he found himself walking along a beach. It was too chilly for there to be many people around, but that didn't stop the surfers that he saw catching waves out in the distance. The memory of when he and Quinn spent a whole day at the beach on Asmaria entered his mind. That was one of his all-time favorite memories now. This beach wasn't nearly as beautiful as the other, but what made it beautiful was Quinn. He wondered if she made it home safely.

Since leaving that forest, he hadn't experienced anything out of the ordinary. Then a seagull landed on his shoulder and pecked at his ear. He swatted the bird away and then screamed his frustration into the open air. The anger welling inside him wasn't the usual indignation that every teenager felt from time to time. It was that old rage that he only felt when things got really bad. The rage he felt just before he was about to explode. Getting a peck on the ear by a random seagull normally wouldn't have set him off, but the past day's events began to overwhelm him.

Ash was breathing heavily, the power inside him building. He looked up into a cloudy sky and roared, clenching his fists as tightly as possible. He felt power release from him, but it didn't come from his hands or any other part of his body this time. The sky crackled and purple lightning struck the ground only 20 feet away from him, leaving behind a small natural sculpture of the glassy crystal that's created when lightning meets sand.

Again, the power was building up inside him. The rage he felt consumed the mild confusion and then lightning struck the sand again and again. Five times this happened until his anger began to fade. The most startling event of the day occurred when a deep voice penetrated his mind, interrupting his thoughts.

Why have you awoken me, boy? The voice didn't sound fully human, but he could understand it clearly. Ash looked around frantically to see who could be doing this but saw no one.

"Who's there? Where are you?" He shouted but no one appeared.

Keeping secrets, eh? The voice reverberated in his head. *Fine. I'll just look for myself.*

Ash fell backward into the sand, paralyzed. Something was pouring through his memories. Every memory of his life was flashing by as if he were reliving each one. It felt like he'd lived another fourteen years all over again, but it was only a couple of seconds. When it was over, Ash fell to the sand and clutched his head. Fear was now gripping him. *What could be doing this to me?*

Me. That voice again. And then the sky split open. A bird at least three times the size of Ash erupted through the clouds. Ash tried crawling backwards but the bird was faster. The wind kicked bits of sand up into Ash's face as it flapped its wings to slow its descent. Ash saw lighting crackling around the bird. It was regal. He wasn't sure if it was awe or terror running through him at the sight of the massive beast.

If not for its immense size, the bird would have looked like a normal falcon. Of course, it was shrouded in arcs of lightning as well. The bird's black eyes were focused on Ash and its razor-sharp talons could have ripped him to shreds at any moment. Despite the creature's terrifying figure, Ash couldn't help but be flabbergasted, utterly awe-stricken, even as the cold hand of fear gripped him as if it were a vice.

You needn't fear me, boy. I have seen your memories and know why you've awakened me. I do apologize for invading your mind. I will only peruse your memories with your permission now. I had to be sure of your intentions before I revealed myself.

"Awaken you?" Ash asked. "I didn't do that. Or, at least I don't remember doing that."

It may have been an accident, but I can only be summoned from my realm by a lightning wielder in times of great need. And I'd say right now, you are in great need, are you not?

"I am. I need to get back to Asmaria. My friends and my home are in trouble."

Yes, indeed. This is not the first time I've dealt with you Asmarians, although, it has been many years. You and I are now bonded. We can hear each other's thoughts from any distance.

So, you can hear this? Ash tested it out.

Yes, the bird said.

Ash laughed, nearly not believing what was happening. *What do I call you?* he asked.

My name is Raimir. I am a protector of lightning, the only one from my realm. I will be your companion until that which threatens your world is eliminated. He continued even though Ash had a bewildered look on his face. *Now then, Ash, son of Augustus, are you ready?*

With determination Ash said, *Let's do it.* Raimir squatted

so Ash could easily climb onto his back. He bent his legs and launched into the air. The speed with which the creature was flying left Ash exhilarated. The ground disappeared within a second and Ash wondered if his face was going to be pulled off by the acceleration.

Ash asked, *Do you think anyone saw you?*

Raimir replied, *it's not something I worry about. Humans see what they want to see. Hear what they wish to hear. Especially those not attuned to the likes of me.*

After a minute or so, Raimir slowed down a bit so that Ash could recover his grip on the bird's feathers. Ash asked him, *So, where did you come from and how is it that I brought you here? I don't remember doing anything out of the ordinary.*

His deep voice rumbled, *I come from a world filled with nothing but great beasts. It is a transcendental plane that no human has yet to enter. I, like many of my kind, am a spiritual creature. We do not know how we were created, only that we have a singular purpose. Answer the call of any great hero who beckons us.*

But I didn't call you. Not that I'm not grateful for you being here, I just don't see how I could have done anything to bring you here. Plus, I'm no hero. I'm more of a failure.

No, you are not a failure. Bringing me here was not anything that you've done directly. It's more like I felt a tugging sensation as I did the last time I entered this world. Your distress was so powerful that I could feel it from my realm, and I followed the feeling. That's what led me to you.

Ash remembered the tugging sensation that he too had felt earlier. Had he gotten over himself, quit the pity party, and just given into the feeling he probably would have been back on Asmaria by now. He mentally kicked himself for constantly being so hard on himself, and the irony of it all was that he was doing it again at that moment. He wanted to stop. He wanted nothing more than to feel confident like he was worth more than his mistakes. If only it were that simple.

Great. So it was my desperation from being separated from my friends.

Ash, it takes courage to admit you need help. If not for your subconscious crying out, you'd still be stuck without a ride to your real home.

Ash pondered all of that; it didn't make a whole lot of sense to him yet, but maybe someday it would. He believed what he said about himself, that he wasn't a hero, but perhaps he would reach that status before all this was over. He wanted to make sure Raimir didn't waste a trip to their world. *Think you can get us there any faster?* He asked.

Want to see some real speed? The bird asked, looking over his shoulder at Ash. *Watch this.*

Lightning crackled and arced around their bodies. They turned into pure lightning and vanished from the sky. The world disappeared in Ash's eyes and he didn't feel the energy move through his body. He *was* the energy. His body had taken the form of lightning and it was amazing. When time slowed back down and his body snapped back to its normal form, Asmaria was a stone's throw away.

The Vision

Ash had fistfuls of the bird's soft feathers as Raimir flew toward the Great Tree. It wasn't in sight for Ash yet, but he heard Raimir's voice in his mind, *It appears that Gethin has been restored to her former glory.*

How do you know her name? And how can you see that far?

How I know her is a story for another time. As for my vision, see for yourself.

Ash didn't know what he meant by that, and the secretive nature of the giant bird was annoying. Before he could tell Raimir that he couldn't see that far, he felt a pulse of energy pass through him and his vision changed. The colors became more vibrant and he could see further. The Great Tree had been healed. Ash couldn't believe how beautiful everything looked.

"Is this how you always see?" Ash asked him.

It is, however, things are different at night. Such as a hawk in your world, I too am a daytime beast. I can't see nearly as well in the dark, but if you happen to need me, I will still be by your side.

The vision cleared and Ash's eyesight went back to normal. They were near the Tree now, coming in for a landing. Once the bird's feet were on the ground Ash dismounted, stretching his back and legs. The flight had made him stiff despite how quickly they got here. It's possible turning into actual lightning was more cumbersome on him than if they were to fly normally.

Ash looked around but didn't see anyone. They must have taken care of getting the elixir here rather quickly. That must mean the Guardians won that battle he saw as they left the island. He felt that everything would be okay from then on. For some reason, Ash was compelled to go touch the Tree. He felt the need to just lay his hand upon it, so he did just that. As soon as his skin touched its bark, his mind was transported elsewhere. His breath caught and he couldn't move.

He was watching the scene before him unravel as if he were watching it from above. He couldn't do anything to stop it or help those about to die. He was floating above a tiny island that was a fraction of the size of Asmaria. It didn't even look to be a mile wide or long. There were hundreds of people gathered; men, women, and children all in attendance gathered around a man. Their garb was entirely black and he knew who they were before he could see any faces.

As his body got closer, he saw the man in the middle wearing that grey mask from the first time he met him. Augustus. He was giving some sort of speech but Ash couldn't hear him yet. As he got within range, the distorted words became audible.

"—and that is why your sacrifice will turn the tide in this war. You will go down in history as the bravest men and women this world has ever known. Stories will be told by the people who remain for centuries to come. Now, kneel." Most of the Forbidden responded earnestly, however, many of them hesitated. They looked uncertain. Their women looked frightened and their children had tears rushing down their cheeks.

Their leader grew impatient. "I said, kneel!" Augustus bellowed the last word which caused the rest to take to the ground. After getting them to their knees, he began chanting something incomprehensible. When his chant was seemingly complete, he said, "Their souls are yours, Master." He spread his arms out and the shadowy figure of Aros, except he looked smaller, emerged from the man's body. Every person in the crowd—except Augustus—was immediately lifted off the ground by an invisible force. Their heads were yanked back and they stiffened as trails of blindingly white energy began to pour from their mouths and were absorbed by the demon king. It only took a couple of seconds and when the energy had all vanished, the Forbidden bodies crashed limply to the ground. Aros had grown double his previous size and was laughing maniacally.

Ash saw his father remove the mask with trembling hands, a look of—perhaps remorse—in his eyes. That look vanished as Aros turned to face him. He knelt, bowing his head to his master. It made Ash sick. The whole scene made him feel like he was going to puke. The last thing he saw was the brightly glowing yellow eyes of Aros as his head was thrown back in laughter.

He was yanked back to his reality and fell to the ground, gasping for air. He turned and saw Raimir studying him. *What happened, boy? You merely touched the Tree for a second.*

Did it happen that fast? To Ash, it had felt like several minutes passed by. "Hold on. You said it's possible to share memories with each other, right?"

It is. Just focus on the memory and imagine you're replaying it for me.

As difficult as it was, Ash did just that. He replayed every grueling detail of that horrible vision and imagined he was transferring the mental images over to Raimir's mind. If a giant bird could look shocked, Raimir appeared to be. *That is... concerning, to say the least,* he said.

"We have to get to my friends. They'll know what to do." Raimir dropped his shoulder and Ash dashed up onto his back. They blasted into the sky and Ash pointed at the Capital, "Go there!" Ash's hair whipped through the roaring wind as they plummeted to the ground. As they approached the street in front of the Guild building, Raimir spread his wings out and they slowed down. His talons scratched the cobblestone street and within half a second, mages popped out from behind buildings. Their eyes glowing and their hands at the ready for a battle.

An angry, threatening screech erupted from Raimir, and his wings spread wide. Lightning crackled all around his massive body and around his wings. Ash jumped up to his feet and yelled, "Wait! Don't attack!" He saw the Guardians step forward along with Rick and his other friends.

"Ash?" Quinn looked relieved to see him. He was for sure relieved to see her. He slid off Raimir's back and ran to her. He didn't care who saw him. He threw his arms around her and she reciprocated the embrace.

"Hey don't steal all the hugging action," he heard Kane say behind her. Ash let go and hugged his friend, "We thought we lost you there, pal."

Ash chuckled, "You did for a second there." He then took a turn hugging Rick and shaking the hands of each Guardian after Avani declined a hug. "I have to tell you guys something important." He told them.

Avani looked over his shoulder at the bird, "Uh, yeah you do. Mind explaining the big bird?" That warranted a sort of hiss from Raimir.

"Oh, yeah. Listen, there are more important things right now. Something terrible is about to happen to the Forbidden. I just had a vision from the Great Tree."

He explained everything he saw and when he'd finished, a man dressed in black stepped out from the crowd. Power immediately ripped through Ash and lightning covered his hands. He'd recognize the Forbidden anywhere, but how this man was here among the mages, Ash didn't know. Before he could act, the Guardians jumped in front of him and Avani held his hands up.

"Easy there, buddy," Avani said. "This is Draven. He deserted the Forbidden and came with information to help us take them down. The vision you just told us about is nearly identical to what he told us was going to happen." The Guardian pinched the bridge of his nose and then said loud enough for all to hear, "Okay. Everyone into the Guild building, now. We have to figure out what's going on."

Draven protested, "We don't have time for this!"

"Listen," Bora interjected, "much has transpired in the past several hours. We need to regroup and organize before anyone makes any more rash decisions. Is that understood?" Ash had never heard her be so firm and direct, but Draven nodded his head and everyone began heading for the Guild building.

Avani turned to Raimir, "Assuming you can understand me, you're not going to fit."

Call my name when you need me. I will be close, he told Ash. *Oh, and tell your friend not to insult my intelligence again.* Then he sprang into the air and disappeared with a flash of lightning.

An attendance sheet was being passed around the crowd; it was important to keep records of all those currently serving in the Guild. The kids stood in front of the Guardians and Draven, explaining everything that had occurred since they left. Ash noted that Kailani was standing next to Kane and only spoke when asked a direct question.

"Why did you ditch Atlantis?" Avani asked her.

"I couldn't stay there anymore. I've wanted to leave for years, but father was adamant that I stay, seeing as I will never be able to return."

Lenna said, "Your father was probably right. We don't know that we will be able to find much use of you here. Perhaps something menial will fit your skillset."

"Ma'am," Kane jumped in, "Kailani is a great warrior. She beat Quinn and me in battle. She also has a way with magical runes, something no one here has yet to discover. Go ahead, show them."

Kailani grabbed a small piece of paper, scribbled an Atlantean rune on it, and muttered something in her native language. The rune glowed and then a flame appeared, burning away the slip of paper.

"Okay," Leena said, "you will join our ranks on a provisional basis. Understood?"

"Yes, ma'am."

Ash saw Kane beaming at that news. The boy was smitten and Ash knew it. He hoped it would all work out for them when this was all over. After that, Ash learned of everything that had transpired until the point of his return. He couldn't believe it. They all were imprisoned for nearly the entire time Ash and the others were off living it up underground. He made a mental note to thank Rick for leading the rescue party that broke them free. The Tree would have died without them showing up when they did. The heala they ate worked wonders for them. Ash had been on the receiving end of needing to heal quickly, and that stuff always quickened the healing process tenfold.

Avani turned to Ash with an eyebrow raised, "So, about the giant bird. Want to explain that?"

Ash told him everything from the moment they left Atlantis and he found himself stranded in front of his old apartment building. How he took down two Forbidden cronies and then wandered the city aimlessly. He told him how he got so angry that lightning burst from the sky, striking the sandy beach he was trekking upon. And then how he had somehow summoned Raimir from his realm. He spared no part of the story, including everything Raimir had told Ash about being a hero and how he unknowingly called out for help. The information that the mystical beast could communicate with Ash telepathically seemed to be the most striking part of the story. When he was done Avani said, "Well, it's certainly a good thing he showed up. I'm sure he will do wonders for us against Aros."

"The first order of business," Bora addressed the Guild as Ash and his friends found their seats, "is to ascertain where your allegiance now lies." She let those words hang in the air for a moment. "In our weakest hour, not one of you came to our side. I get it, you were probably scared and didn't know what to do. And then a few of you were able to break us free and the rest of you *continued* to believe that these kids were trying to kill the Great Tree. Do you understand what would have happened if we hadn't shown up in time? We had to be saved by the one person on this island who wasn't born here!"

Ash looked around and saw regret in many pairs of eyes. Downcast faces and some streaming tears were popular among the crowd. He didn't pity them in the slightest. Whatever punishment they get is what they deserve. He knew they needed warriors, but he hoped they were imprisoned or banished. Just to see how they like it. The thought made him smirk and then he realized how dark that was. *What is wrong with me?*

"With that being said, we are giving you all two options. One: you leave Asmaria and never return. If you believe that these kids are traitors and that we are as well, even after all we've done to save our home, then you don't deserve to call yourself an Asmarian. Option two: accept our forgiveness and vow to never act in this manner again." A few relieved sobs rang out and she continued. "Dark days lie ahead for us. We are at war still and we are willing to look past what you've done as long as you're willing to fight at our sides once again." A few excited shouts were made and Bora chuckled.

"Our new friend here, Draven, has brought news from the Forbidden. That which he has fled in hopes of destroying the brotherhood that he was a part of. The floor is yours." Bora yielded to allow Draven a chance to speak.

He stepped forward, "My parents died in the battle at Birkwood Park last year. I wasn't there, and I felt angry at first. I even worked my way up to being Augustus' right-hand man. Then I realized how evil our organization is. I waited for an opportunity to kill him myself, but it never came. And then I overheard the most awful plan they've ever come up with and rushed here to tell you all. Hopefully, we haven't used up too much time and we can stop them." Draven proceeded to share everything he heard his leaders say as he eavesdropped on them. His story corroborated the vision that Ash saw.

When there were murmurs of disbelief rustling through the assembly, Avani took the floor. "It's true. Ash told us of a vision he had at the Great Tree before he even heard this story from Draven. Aros means to drain the souls of every Forbidden member to regain his strength. If we can stop this from happening, we may just be able to kill that demon for good. We may even save the Forbidden from a life of darkness."

Draven noticed that they weren't leaving him unattended. He knew they didn't fully trust him; maybe they trusted him enough to try stopping Aros before he killed all those people, but not enough to let him have a moment alone on their island. He wanted so badly to go see that Tree again though. He knew he'd be able to slip away at night. The shadows were his ally and he had learned how to hide in them a long time ago. The one called Avani had been keeping an eye on him, but he got distracted while they were making battle plans, so Draven took his opportunity.

He snuck away, running through the night towards the Tree. He remembered where it was from seeing it earlier. He was fast, and the shadows made him faster. He was there within minutes. The glorious sight of it left him astonished. It was magnificent. Draven had no intention to act ill toward the Tree. He crept towards it, simply taking in its beauty.

"Good evening," a voice behind him startled him from his wonderment. He spun around with his heart beating rapidly; he'd been caught. The kid with white hair stood in front of him, the moon making it look like his head was glowing.

"I was just trying to look at it."

"I believe you. You know, all you had to do was ask. However, sneaking away like that sure does make you look suspicious."

The kid took a step toward him.

Draven didn't have his powers right now. It had been far too long since he siphoned energy from the obelisk and he was now defenseless. He was getting scared now. He knew this kid was incredibly strong and there was no way he'd survive a fight against him. He began walking backward, only a few feet away from the Tree.

"Hey, what are you doing? Get away—" The boy lunged forward with his arm stretched out. He grabbed the lapel of Draven's robes just as his back slammed into the Tree and the scene in his eyes shifted.

He and the white-haired boy were in a world that was completely devoid of color, and yet they could still see each other clearly. The boy still held onto his robes, letting go as he looked around at their surroundings. "Where are we?" Draven asked.

"It's a vision. The Great Tree does this from time to time, although, I have no clue what she would want to say to *you*."

"She?"

"Yes, she." That voice. It was like a thousand voices wrapped into one. It sounded ethereal. A small flying human-like creature appeared. Her beauty left Draven speechless. "My name is Gethin. I am the entity known here as the Great Tree. I am what protects and gives out magic based on how I see fit."

So, it was her fault that he and the other Forbidden members were born without ever developing magic? Now he was mad. He seethed, "You. It's your fault I'm like this!"

"Calm yourself, Draven." *How does she know my name?* "Everything happens for a reason. You were born for a reason. You fled your brotherhood for a reason. And now you are here for a reason. I want to ask you something."

"Okay," he said. "Go ahead."

"If I were to grant you a magical ability, how would you use it? Would you use it for your gain? Would you turn to the evil ways? Or would you wield it with the responsibility of protecting people?"

Is she considering giving powers to me? "Ma'am, um, Gethin, please I'd do anything to have powers. It's all I've ever really wanted. I swear to you, I'll take down Aros myself if you give me the ability to wield."

She seemed to consider his words. "Very well. I believe you are already familiar with the shadows." She smirked and said, "It is done. Now go, before you're too late to stop him." The environment began to fade and then she spoke to the kid who'd been silent the whole time, "Oh, and Kane? Be sure to tell your Guardians that Draven has my full trust." Kane nodded and everything went back to normal. Kane let go of Draven's robes.

"Shadows huh?" Kane asked and then, "Go ahead, try it out."

Draven curled his right hand and a shadow that was darker than the night around them issued from the ground. Then it poked Kane in the arm and disappeared as if it were never there. Draven's mouth curled into a smile and he laughed, "Oh this is going to be so cool."

Sunset Crest

Draven spent roughly an hour being berated by the Guardians regarding his disappearance. Lucky for him, Kane witnessed everything and was able to back up his story, including the vision given to them by Gethin. They explained every detail and Draven showed the Guardians how he could now wield shadows at will without needing assistance from Aros.

After everyone had calmed down, Draven said, "Let's go! We're wasting time here. There's no telling when Aros is going to kill all of my people. I still have friends there, good people who don't deserve this!"

"We're not charging in there with no plan," Avani told him. "That's the kind of thing that gets our people killed. We need to develop some sort of strategy and then we will do what we can to save your people."

Draven was fuming. He turned away and stomped off in the opposite direction. Kane caught up and said, "Hey, how about we go get some training in?"

"Training?" Draven asked. "Why would I want to do that?"

"Come on, it's fun. I'm sure you could use some work on your combat skills."

Draven was feeling insulted. Who did this kid think he was talking to? He'd been in plenty of fights before. He could hold his own, that much he was sure of. "Sure," he said with a sly smile. "Let's go have some fun."

Kane led him to the training field where there were a few people already gathered to do some sparring. He saw the boy named Ash boxing with a silver-haired girl, and a blonde one watching nearby. The metaphorical golden child that Aros wanted to get his hands on so desperately. He had his chance, but he blew it. None of the other Forbidden members were there to witness what had occurred, but even with their fear of Aros, the rumors still spread.

"Hey, Ash. How about you get a few rounds in with our new friend here?" Kane asked him.

Draven was once again feeling insulted. He may have been young, but he was tall and strong. Not only did Kane want to spar, but now he was delegating it to the smaller kid. Draven laughed, "Really? Am I the only one who sees the mismatch here? I'm much bigger than him."

Ash answered, "You should take me down pretty easily then, right?"

Okay. If that's how they wanted to do things, Draven would oblige. He took a fighting stance and the two began circling each other. Draven planned on playing around with him, but his plans changed when the boy came at him with a surprising ferocity. The kid was a whole head shorter than Draven, but what he lacked in size, he made up for with speed and technique.

All Draven could do was dodge and block the punches that were raining down on him and he was barely able to do that. Ash struck him with a push kick to the stomach which created some distance between the two and Draven was ready when he charged him. Ash came in with a flying side kick, but Draven caught his leg as he spun away and flung him to the ground. Now was his chance to win.

He jumped on top of the boy and pulled his arm back, fist clenched. Before he could drop it onto the boy's face, he bucked his hips up and Draven lost his balance. Ash took advantage of the momentum and rolled him over to his back. Draven grasped desperately for anything he could hold onto, but Ash was already moving past his legs. Ash cleared Draven's hips and thrust his knee into the man's belly, pinning him to the ground. The pressure was nearly unbearable. He wondered how such a small kid could feel so heavy.

Draven pushed against the kid's knee, a feeble attempt to escape the encumbrance. Air flooded Draven's lungs as the force lifted from his stomach. Ash spun around, trapping Draven's arm between his legs. He fell back, thrusting his hips upward into Draven's elbow. It was going to break if he didn't yield. But how could he be so humiliated as yielding to this boy?

He pulled at the energy that was building in him. As his arm was starting to give, a shadow sprang to life and wrapped around Ash's throat. The boy let go of Draven's arm and he jumped to his feet. As soon as he was upright, there was a dagger to his throat and he heard a girl's voice behind him, "Let him go. Now." The shadow disappeared with a wave of his hand and Ash gasped for air.

The blonde girl moved around to Ash's side to see if he was okay. Suddenly, Draven was embarrassed. He'd let his fear take over him and reacted poorly. "I'm… I'm sorry about that. I don't know what came over me."

Ash stood, brushing himself off, "Don't worry about it. I don't mean to come after your pride or anything, but you're always welcome to train with us. I know we're all still teenagers but we've been through a lot. You may think of us as ordinary kids, but it's simply not true."

"Thanks," Draven said. "I appreciate that. I think for now, I'm going to try getting some rest."

Draven was glad he decided to flee the Forbidden. Being an Asmarian would be way more fulfilling for him. Safer too. Perhaps he would it in around there after all. Now he just needed to do something about those robes. He was sick of everyone looking at him like he was a criminal.

It had been several months since Quinn and Ash had gotten to spend any time alone. She missed just being around him for the sake of being around him. Lately, it felt like they hardly spoke and were both just solely fixated on beating Aros. They were still so young and she felt they deserved a break. Quinn knew that Ash was too anxious to ask her out on a proper date and she was tired of waiting for him to "man up". Quinn would take matters into her own hands.

"Can you help me with something?" She asked Kailani.

"Sure. What's up?"

"I need you to distract Kane so that I can be alone with Ash for a bit."

Kailani's eyebrows shot up and she smiled, "Alone time with that boy of yours?"

Her cheeks got hot and she knew they had turned red. She shouldn't be embarrassed, but maybe it was only because they weren't *actually* going out. "Well, I wouldn't exactly call him my boy. We've had a few very nice moments together. Even held hands a time or two but we've never talked about it. It's not necessarily official I guess."

Kailani sighed, "In Atlantean culture, we marry once and never again. I constantly had boys trying to gain favor with me, but I couldn't take them seriously. How was I supposed to know if they were being genuine, or just trying to marry into the royal family?"

"Is that why you've taken such a liking to Kane?" Quinn asked.

She nodded, "Yes. He's the first boy who showed interest in me that I knew was genuine. I knew that he wasn't trying to gain access to the throne."

"And that's why you left? If you don't mind me asking, of course."

Her expression saddened, "That's only part of it." A single tear streaked down her cheek, "I just… couldn't continue living with my path in life already determined for me. I'm 16 years old and have never seen the actual sun before. If it had been higher in the sky when we appeared, I probably would have been blinded. Being treated like royalty but not doing anything to deserve the crown except being born into the family? I mean… I couldn't do that! Father will live longer than me now that I've left. The anti-aging spell will not have followed me. And then there's the issue of this world being destroyed. He would sit idly by and do nothing! He cares more about letting you Asmarians fight the demon on your own, but not me. I'm going to do everything I can to help, and if we lose, then I can die knowing that I didn't hide underground."

"Wow," Quinn said. "That was a lot to take in."

Kailani laughed, "Thank you for asking. I needed to get that off my chest. Now, back to your problem. Of course, I'll help you. It shouldn't be too difficult to get Kane's attention. He has a *major* crush on me." She chuckled.

"How can you tell?" Quinn asked.

"The boy can't take his eyes off me. Look, here they come." Quinn turned to where she nodded and the two boys were coming their way. Ash was as handsome as ever, more even. He was getting taller and now stood several inches above her. He had a new confidence about him since arriving on the giant lightning bird. She desperately wanted more information about that.

"Evening, ladies," Kane said cooly.

"Come with me," Kailani said as she grabbed him by the wrist and led him away. She looked over her shoulder at Quinn who mouthed a 'thank you'.

"Want to take a walk?" She asked Ash.

"Sure. Just let me tell Rick that I'll be out for a while." They walked in the direction of their homes since they were nearly right next to each other. They popped in and greeted Rick. The man was pouring over books that Quinn recognized as Asmarian history books. He hardly looked up as Ash told him he'd be going out. The man must have been fully immersed in learning as much about her people as he could.

The two walked together through the city streets as the sun began to drop. She knew where she wanted to go; it was one of the best spots to watch the sun dip beneath the sky. They called it Sunset Crest and she was just hoping no one else had shown him that place yet. The only other person she knew he spent time with was Kane, but that boy was almost as likely as she was to show off this particular piece of scenery.

"Where are we going?" Ash asked her.

"It's only the most beautiful sight around here," she said. "Just wait, you'll thank me later."

She saw the corners of his mouth curve up slightly as he said, "The most beautiful sight around is wherever you are." And then her heart was suddenly beating rapidly, her stomach was doing somersaults. Did he just say that? She'd always gotten the sense that he was nervous around her, but with a single sentence, he'd betrayed that notion.

Quinn couldn't help but smile. "That was really sweet, and rather uncharacteristic of you. I *do* appreciate it though."

He chuckled, "Yeah, that took a lot of courage for me to say, although I've been wanting to say something like that for a while. It's just hard—"

"To express yourself?" She interrupted.

"Exactly."

She took his hand in hers and they continued walking until the massive boulder came into view and they began to climb. It wasn't too steep to traverse without hands, but it would leave a lesser-fit person breathing hard. As they reached the top he asked, "Ice magic, huh? I haven't seen you do that yet."

She lifted her palm and summoned a swirling ball of water and then focused more intently, just as before. She had practiced a few times, but it was harder than her usual water magic. The first time she did it, it was only so successful because of her heightened emotions. The emblem on her arm glowed and then the ball of water finally solidified. She dropped the ball of ice which shattered on the hard rock.

"That's awesome," he said with a wide smile. And then, "So what is this place? I've learned Asmaria has a name for everything."

"This is Sunset Crest," she told him. "I used to come here with my mom when I was little. It's the best place to watch the sun go down."

"It is a stunning sight," Ash said, taking it all in.

They sat down, their legs just barely touching, but it was enough for Quinn to take notice. She didn't dare move. As the sun descended, the sky transformed into a canvas painted with a palette of warm hues. The soft, golden glow bathed the surroundings in a warm embrace. As the minutes passed, the colors intensified, creating a spectacle of oranges, pinks, purples, and reds that danced across the sky. It was a brilliant display put on by nature that Quinn found herself transfixed by as the day transitioned to night. The sun sank out of sight and left a lingering glow across the horizon. When her trance ended, she noticed Ash looking at her.

"There's something I've been wanting to do for a long time now," he said. "I just didn't know how to go about it. So, I'm just going to go for it." He shrugged and slowly reached over, grabbing her hand. She thought she felt a slight shake in his palm as he leaned in slowly. Her heart was about to leap out of her chest. She didn't know what happened, but instead of leaning into him, she pulled away. The hurt look that flashed across his face was unmistakable. "Sorry, I—" he muttered before jumping to his feet.

Quinn tried to stop him, "Ash, wait!" But he was already down the rock and onto the ground before she could get to her feet. She slammed her face into her trembling hands. *Why did I do that?* She accosted herself for being so dumb. She liked Ash and wanted to be his girlfriend, but she got so scared realizing that she was about to have her first kiss. She wasn't scared that it was going to be with Ash, or anything like that. She was just worried that she would suck at it. What if he kissed her and then realized she was so bad at it that he'd rather not go out with her? The humiliation of that would be horrible, but if their friendship dwindled because of it, that would be unthinkable.

Ash sprinted faster than he thought possible, the nausea rising in his throat making it even harder to breathe. *Why did I do that?* Ash berated himself for not finding out how she truly felt before attempting such an arduous task. Of course, now he was certain he knew how she felt, he just had to learn the hard way. He wanted to be with her, but it was clear that she didn't reciprocate those feelings.

It didn't matter now, nothing did. He was so embarrassed that he thought this could possibly be the worst thing that had happened to him in his life so far. That included the time he'd zapped Rick with lightning and almost killed him last year. They joked about that now as if it was a hilarious prank, and he hoped that he'd someday be able to joke about the time he'd tried kissing Quinn but she rejected him. Just as he thought it couldn't get any worse, it did.

The roots of a tree protruded on the path he was running on, but he couldn't see that well, not even with the help of the flaming torches along the way. Their faint glow wasn't enough to allow him to fully see the ground. He tripped and the ground found his chin within an instant. He didn't feel anything at first and only blacked out for a few seconds. He stood up and rubbed his chin, pulling back wet fingers. *Great,* he thought. *I'm bleeding again.* He was always bleeding for one reason or another these days.

Ash took his shirt off and pressed it to his chin to stem the flow of blood. He continued down the path, walking this time and careful to watch where he stepped. He just didn't want Quinn to catch up with him; the shame he already felt that night was enough without having to face her again so soon. He didn't know what was in store for them now, but he knew it was going to be awkward. By misreading the situation he may have not only lost a potential girlfriend, but a regular friend as well. That was the last thing he thought could have happened that night.

As Ash came back out into the city streets, he reached out with his mind, *Raimir, I need you if you're free. It's not urgent though.*

The sky split open and lightning lit up the nearby buildings. The giant falcon-like creature floated down to Ash, the wind from his wings causing Ash's hair to ruffle. *I can smell your blood. Are you hurt?* He asked Ash.

No, I'm fine. I've had worse, he tried to reassure his new protector. *I just need to get out of here for a bit if that's okay.*

Of course. Climb on. We'll circle the island until you're ready to come back.

Thank you. Ash tied his bloodied shirt around his waist and climbed up onto Raimir's back. The bird launched off the ground and the island shrank within a couple of seconds. They floated slowly around the outskirts of the island. Ash could see the moon reflecting off the waters of the surrounding waters and the soft glow of the flames around the Capital. The wind and altitude spread chills across his bare chest.

Would you like to talk about what's happened? Raimir's voice rumbled in his head.

Have you ever had a girlfriend? Ash asked.

There was a deep rumble of laughter, *I'm afraid that my kind does not need such things. We do not mate for it is not necessary for us to live. We are created out of necessity and that rings true for all the beings in my realm.*

Ash thought that sounded sort of sad. They would never

have a family, but maybe the creatures in his world were all friends. *I can tell what you're thinking,* Raimir said. *And I've never been lonely. The beings in my world do not need what you would call friends or family. However, if it makes you feel better, you can consider yourself a part of my family. I am here of my own free will after all.*

That came as a surprise to him. *So you're not here just because I needed you? I'm not somehow forcing you into protecting me?*

No. I heard the call of your subconscious, but I alone decided to come to your aid. You are not in control of me, just as I am not in control of you. We are each masters of our own wills. I can see the brightness of your potential, however, and that vastly influenced my decision to stay around.

I'm very thankful for you, Raimir. Ash felt a vibration issue from the beast that had the likeness of a cat's purr. He proceeded to tell him about what had just happened with Quinn, even though he may not understand it, the bird was highly intelligent and was able to give him advice.

I will say that you shouldn't have run away. Running from our problems is hardly ever a good answer to them. It is important to voice your thoughts and feelings, especially to those you care about. The next time you see Quinn, apologize for your brashness. Tell her how you really feel, and if she doesn't reciprocate, then you can move on.

You know, he said, *you're pretty knowledgeable on this subject for someone who has never dated a lady bird.*

A laugh reverberated in Ash's head and Raimir dove back down toward Ash's home. He thanked him for everything again and felt that he'd be thanking him for things until the day they parted ways. When he got inside, Rick was asleep on the coffee table which was littered with tomes still. He pulled him back onto the couch and covered him with the throw blanket, then proceeded to his bed where he would have the recurring nightmare of the Forbidden having their souls absorbed by Aros.

Youthful Advice

Several days had gone by since Draven arrived in Asmaria; he was growing tired of waiting on the Guardians to decide whether they would attempt to rescue the other Forbidden members or not. He still had friends there that he did not wish to see dead. There were many children in their ranks who didn't deserve to be victims of that demon's cruel plans. It was time to seek counsel with the Asmarian leaders.

He met them in Bora's office, the other Guardians standing around in a makeshift circle. Bora offered him some herbal tea, but he declined. He wasn't interested in pleasantries, at the moment he was business only. "Something has to be done. What more convincing do you need? I've told you the plans that Aros and Augustus have made. Your wonder boy Ash has told you of the vision given to him by Gethin. It's only a matter of time before the remaining Forbidden is gathered, and they all die. I will not allow it to happen!" His anger was peaking as they stared at him, seemingly emotionless.

"Draven," Bora said. "We have discussed amongst ourselves about what to do. We still aren't entirely sure that it's a good idea. This could all be a trap. Admittedly, that's one of the less likely things to happen, but it needs consideration. If we decide to defend your friends, we can't just charge in there without a battle plan."

"They won't be expecting us. What more battle plan could you need? The element of surprise is a great tool in a fight." Draven was becoming more impatient. He needed them to see that he was right.

"How many battles have you been in?" She asked.

He knew where this was going. "None."

"Exactly. We know what we're doing. Just be patient. Once we've settled on a decision we'll let you know."

"We don't have time for this!" Draven felt that his head was going to explode. The shadows being cast around the room from the sunlight pouring in began to curl in toward the Guardians. Draven was seething.

"Calm down, Draven. Or this conversation will end with you being hurt." Leena told him. Her gaze locked on him and water swirled around her hands. He forced a deep breath through his nose and the shadows retreated to their original place. He stood up and stormed out of the office, down the halls, and burst through the doors of the Guild building.

He needed to burn off some energy and let off a little steam so he headed for the training field. There were always people at the training field beating each other up. It didn't matter which end of a beating he was on, he just needed it.

Draven found a group of people who looked similar to his age; they looked apprehensive—no doubt because of his black shirt and pants—as he introduced himself. Pretty much everyone knew about him now, but he knew he hadn't earned anyone's trust yet. He wanted to change that. Maybe this was a small step toward earning a little credence from the people he planned to spend the rest of his life around.

They agreed to just spar without magic for now and began. It was much different from sparring with those kids. Ash and his friends were extremely talented and Draven found that he was able to hold his own against these guys. *Those kids are true prodigies.* The guy he was sparring delivered a powerful punch to Draven's mouth and he smiled through bloodied teeth.

Ash still hadn't recovered from the blow that Quinn dealt to his confidence. He was usually up and out of the house by sunrise, however, he couldn't find the strength to move his limbs at the moment. It was so uncharacteristic of him that Rick came in to check on him.

"Anything you want to talk about?" Rick asked after the boy told him he wasn't going to move all day.

Ash wasn't sure if Rick would be able to help him or not; he knew the man had never married so he wasn't sure how much experience he had in the realm of dating. He decided to tell him what happened anyway. Telling him the story was like reliving it all over again. This time, however, his pillow got wet with his tears. Rick walked over and sat on the edge of his bed.

"Ya know, I'm not what anyone would consider a 'lady's man,'" that comment made Ash snicker, "but I remember what girls were like when I was a younger man. They can't be that different now even if we are on a mystical island."

He waited but Ash didn't respond so he continued, "It's often hard to know what a girl is thinking, or anyone for that matter. We can't truly know what's going on in someone's head unless they tell us. Communication is key to any relationship. If you're direct with her and tell her how you feel, you'll feel much better than if you just bury your emotions."

Ash asked, "But what if she doesn't like me? What if I've imagined everything this whole time and she rejects me again?"

The man pondered that for a minute. "You shouldn't fear rejection, Ash. It happens to all of us from time to time. The worst thing she can say is no, and if she does, you can move on with your life and stop worrying about what could have been."

Ash chuckled, "You sound a lot like Raimir."

"I still can't believe you accidentally summoned a giant lightning bird from another dimension," Rick laughed, shaking his head.

"What can I say? I'm a boy of mystery."

"Now *that* we can both agree on," Rick got up and moved to the door. "Let me know if you need anything. I'll always be here for you, whether it's for advice or you just need to vent."

"Thanks, Rick."

"Love ya, kid."

"Love you too." And then he was gone.

Ash wasn't ready to confront Quinn yet, however, he was ready to get out of bed. He completed the laborious task of rolling off his mattress, washed his face, and got dressed. The sun hit his face and his mood instantly shifted. It was amazing what a little sunlight could do for someone in a stupor. Now he just needed to figure out what to do with himself for the day. Rick was no doubt at work already; he'd been allowed to work in a small café where they sold different Asmarian cuisines.

He wasn't hungry and didn't feel like training at the moment. *Maybe I'll just do some hiking.* He set off through the jungle, wandering aimlessly. It didn't matter where his feet took him for there was only so far that the island would allow him to trek. He hardly noticed the head-sized butterflies with vibrant-colored wings floating around him. He was completely lost in thought.

The gears in Ash's mind were ever turning, trying to come up with the best words to say to Quinn the next time he saw her. Would the words come out angry, sad, or hurt? He didn't know for sure. Scenarios played over and over in his head; it was like watching a movie with himself and Quinn as the main actors. Ash professing his true feelings for her in one way or another. He couldn't imagine what it would be like for her to reciprocate those feelings, but he could vividly imagine the rejections. That was probably because he'd already lived through one of them.

Ash didn't realize the familiar path in which he walked until the beach came into view. It was the very same beach Quinn had taken him to. He had visited this place semi-frequently, but none of those times compared to when he was there with Quinn. A few other Asmarians were milling about the sand, and some swimming around just offshore. He saw a water mage nearly decimate her friend with a huge wave of water, although he came up laughing and unharmed.

There was a large rock jutting up from the water a few feet from the shoreline and Ash decided that looked like the perfect spot to soak up some sun. He tossed his shirt onto a nearby log, and trod through the hot sand. He sat down on the rock, leaning back with his hands crossed behind his head, and closed his eyes. The cool water bathed his feet, almost up to his knees. A poking sensation in his foot caused him to sit up abruptly.

Ash looked down just in time to see a chameleon crab scurry across the sand. They were infamous for being able to blend in with their surroundings. Ash could only see it now because the sandy color it had taken on didn't match as it fled. Movement caught the corner of his eye and Ash looked over to see Kane and Kailani walking towards him.

"What's up, bud?" Kane asked him.

"Just needed to clear my head," Ash answered. "What are you guys up to?" Ash knew that Kane was smitten with the girl. He didn't blame him; Kailani was seriously cool and very pretty. Plus, their hair almost matched. It was the craziest coincidence.

"Just showing her the sights of Asmaria."

"I could never imagine how beautiful this place is," she said. "I mean, I saw plenty of painted pictures in our record books, but all those were made from my father's memory. They don't do your home justice."

Ash asked her, "If we survive this war, do you think he'll ever come out from underground?"

He must have asked the wrong question based on how her eyes darkened, "I do not believe he will. He is a coward." She stormed off further into the water and the waves began to part for her, allowing her to walk on damp sand.

Ash was taken aback. He looked at Kane, "How the—" he began, but Kane interrupted. "Yeah, she has this weird way about water. She hasn't learned how to control it, but when her emotions spike it reacts. She's been sort of uptight about the topic of her father lately. I've tried getting her to open up about it, but she hasn't been in much of a talking mood."

"Well," Ash said, "apart from that, you two seem to be getting pretty close. Is it official yet?"

Kane smiled, "I'm not supposed to tell anyone, but I can trust you, so that's a yes." Ash hadn't thought his smile could get any wider, and yet it did. "She's awesome, man. Every time I learn something new about her I'm just left feeling even more lucky that I get to be her boyfriend. What about you and Quinn? Everyone can tell that you two are into each other. I've known for a while that you like each other."

He just had to go there. Ash's stomach twisted into a knot and he laid back down on the rock with a huff. "I don't even know. She kind of… rejected me once already. I don't think she's as into me as you think. I do like her though. I've known I wanted to be with her since the moment we met. I just don't think it's going to happen."

"You'll never know unless you try," Kane said. "I believe everything happens for a reason. And if things are meant to be, then they will be. If not, they won't. You better find out where she stands before it's too late though. Some other lucky guy is going to come in and sweep her off her feet."

"That's pretty profound for a kid," Ash responded.

"Hey man, I'm 17 now. I'm practically an adult," Kane said with a sly grin.

The waves were parting as Kailani returned, her face not showing the anger that it had when she disappeared into the water. She looked at Ash, "Sorry about that. I get a little worked up talking, or even thinking about my father keeping our people hidden underground. I haven't quite got the hang of my emotions yet."

Kane put his arm around her shoulders and she wrapped her arm around his waist, laying her head on his shoulder. She seemed to realize what she was doing because her eyes went wide and she jumped back, glaring at Kane. He laughed, "It's okay. I told him. Ash won't say anything."

"Honestly," Ash said, "your secret's safe with me. Although I don't know why you'd want to keep this gorgeous goof a secret."

She chuckled, "I've never dated anyone. I just don't want your people thinking that he's the only reason I followed you."

"But that is the only reason," Kane joked. Kailani responded by punching him in the arm, making him wince.

"I came because I believed the right thing to do is help in any way possible." Ash respected her for that.

"Well, either way," Ash said, "we're all glad you're here, and I'm happy for the two of you. It takes a special girl to keep this guy from his training."

Kane looked down at her as he pulled her back into his arms and said, "She's worth it." Kailani didn't have a response to that besides a bright smile. *He's going to make the girl melt,* Ash thought.

"Okay," Ash said, "I better get back and figure out what I'm going to say to her."

"Quinn, I assume?" Kailani asked. Ash nodded his head and she told him, "I can tell she likes you."

A bit of hope struck his heartstrings, "How can you tell?"

"It's a girl thing. Just trust me," she told him.

"Okay, but if I get rejected again, I'm blaming you."

A nervous look crossed her gaze, "Rejected again?" Ash declined to answer but he knew Kane would probably tell her. He was already jogging away, turning slightly to wave goodbye. He had work to do.

Joining The Fight

Thaoc hadn't always been the largest man around; he was born smaller than the average Atlantean. His survival was never assured, and in fact, friends of his parents didn't believe he would live past the age of ten, simply because he was so small. In those days, life for an Atlantean was much rougher. Luckily, he lived and prospered. His body took on a growth that surpassed every Atlantean alive. He was the biggest among his people. By the age of 16 he'd outgrown the normal size and his clothing, armor, and weapons had to be crafted to fit his enormous frame.

The normal-sized swords and spears were nearly too small to fit his hands, too light for him to throw accurately. Atlantis' people are among some of the first civilizations ever created. Their people are the oldest living groups in this world. Thaoc was one of the oldest warriors among the Atlanteans; he'd been in more than one battle. The hammer of Ogun—which he wielded—was his greatest asset. Magic was often used against the Atlanteans in the old days and the hammer was essential to keeping Thaoc and many of his comrades alive.

Now he readied for battle yet again. He thought he'd never see a real fight again. The tournaments at the Atlanteum had grown old for him and many others, although they didn't have the heart to break the news to their King.

He strapped the laces of his sandals and put on his armor as his best friend, Mirdok, did the same at his side. The two men had grown up together. Mirdok was always bigger until the year of Thaoc's immense growth spurt. "Well, old friend," Mirdok said, "looks like we will see battle together one last time after all."

Thaoc nodded, "Indeed." He smiled sadly. Everyone knew that the powerful spell keeping them from aging would lose its effect once they breached the wards of their underground kingdom. King Gabriel had given everyone the choice of staying or going. To stay would mean they would never have the chance to resurface and would spend the rest of their days down here. To go would mean your aging would resume. Thaoc and his friend looked to be in their mid-thirties so they probably had quite a few years left. As for the elders, however, they are the eldest of the Atlanteans and their natural time would be up much sooner.

Still, not a single Atlantean chose to stay. King Gabriel had been a fair and kind ruler to them in his time, and they all trusted him and his decisions. When his daughter fled with the Asmarians, the King was livid. The ground shook when he smashed his mighty trident into it. After he calmed down, he called for a gathering in his palace to discuss what to do.

When Thaoc heard of a coming war with an evil being who planned to conquer the Earth, he immediately wanted to support the Asmarians. Many agreed, but it seemed there were just as many who believed otherwise, those who thought it wasn't their problem, not their war. Thaoc knew the right path would be to fight alongside them, but he would listen to whatever the King declared. Then he offered the choice, and it was much to Thaoc's surprise that no one opted to stay in their kingdom where they would most likely live forever, as long as they won the war of course.

"What do you think the surface is like now?" Thaoc asked Mirdok.

The man chuckled, "I figure it's going to be blinding."

"That's probably true. We haven't seen sunlight in ages."

Thaoc couldn't remember how old he was, but a youthful excitement coursed his veins. It wouldn't be long now. They were to meet in the Atlanteum after gathering only the essentials. He had a couple of changes of clothes, waterskins, and various rations in his pack. He was ready to go. Adrenaline pumped through him as he and his friend walked toward the rendezvous point. There were many people in front and behind him heading in the same direction. He just hoped they weren't too late to be of help.

He entered the Atlanteum and marched straight over to the King, taking a knee with his head bowed. The head of his hammer was placed on the ground. "I am ready for battle, my Lord," he said.

"Rise, Thaoc," King Gabriel ordered. "I am glad to have you as my General once again. I know that I can trust you to lay waste to our enemies. You are our mightiest warrior." He placed a hand on the giant's shoulder as he stood.

"No, great King. That would be you," Thaoc said with a chuckle.

"You're too kind, old friend." Thaoc saw the King's eyes darken. "I do not know what lies ahead for our people. If I am to pass on, I want you to take my place. You would make a great ruler."

Thaoc was shocked, to say the least. "My King… I don't know what to say."

"Say nothing for now. Let us hope that it doesn't come to that." He turned, looking around for someone, "Now then, where is the shaman?"

Thaoc couldn't imagine himself as the King of Atlantis. He wasn't sure he'd be good at making the big decisions. All he'd ever been good at is killing and now he was about to do some more of that. Politics was never a topic of interest to him, only getting stronger and deadlier.

Farmers began entering the Atlanteum, struggling to calm their livestock. The animals appeared to be nervous after being taken from their usual enclosures. The leaders of agriculture were charged with gathering up all the livestock and enough supplies to sustain them for a while. This journey would be rough on the entire kingdom, but it was necessary.

King Gabriel's voice called out, "Atlanteans! The shamans are prepared to take us to the surface. This spell is similar to that which took the Asmarians back to their homeland, however, we are too many to travel such a great distance. You need not do anything besides prepare yourselves, for very soon we will be reunited with the surface world." Cheers rang out all around Thaoc.

A bit of nervousness ran through him. It didn't last long, just until his eyes found his wife, Carel. Their gazes connected and she gave him a reassuring nod. They had a simple marriage and she was a warrior like him. She was the most beautiful creature he'd ever seen and no one could convince him otherwise. She was barren so they never had children, but Thaoc was okay with that. He wasn't sure what kind of father he would have been anyway. They held their gaze with each other, even after the shaman began chanting, and even after their bodies began to glow.

Thaoc only felt the cold sensation and saw the pitch-black darkness for a couple of seconds before the surface world was thrust upon him. It was either daybreak or sunset, he couldn't tell which, but he was ever grateful that the sun wasn't at its high point. Even with the light fading he had to squint and saw those around him doing the same. His wife found him, throwing her arms around his waist and he returned the embrace.

Mirdok appeared beside them, inhaled a deep breath, and said, The man let loose a long sigh, breathing in the fresh air. "I can't believe we're back to the surface."

"I never would have thought we'd return either, old friend," Thaoc responded. "Are you excited, my love?"

Carel looked up at him, a glimmer of hope in her cobalt blue eyes, "Wherever you go, I will follow." Thaoc could hear shouts of command from the front of their caravan as they began to walk. "What is our next step?" Carel asked him.

"We must find the ocean," Thaoc told her.

When a Bad Idea Sounds Good

Draven was at his breaking point. He refused to wait any longer for the Guardians to make a move to stop Aros. If they were too cowardly to act then he would take matters into his own hands. He knew none of the other Guild members would follow him; their trust in him was minuscule, to say the least. He made his move as the sun was just past noon. The young man was rife with confidence and bravado, thanks to his new abilities. He would've been more powerful in the dark, but so would Aros and Augustus.

His biggest advantage was the element of surprise. If they were gathering all the Forbidden, Draven knew one of two things to be true. Either they would be waiting for him to show up, or they would see that he wasn't coming. Either way, he'd have to wait until the last possible second to make his move. He just hoped that he wasn't too late.

He was stomping past the training field when he saw Ash walking in his direction, smiling as he noticed him. *Not this kid again,* Draven thought. "Hey, Draven. Where ya headed?" Ash asked him.

Draven didn't need the boy bothering him right now. "Look, I'm in a hurry, so if you don't mind I'd like to be on my way."

He pushed past the kid, determined to not be deterred in the slightest from his mission.

He heard Ash jogging behind him to catch up. The boy got around in front of him, walking backward, and said, "If you need help with something, I'd be happy to lend a hand. I'm kind of looking for something to take my mind off other… things." This might just be what Draven needed. Even though Ash was just a teenager, he was strong and capable, probably the strongest mage here. With training, he would be for sure, but Draven didn't have time to waste. It was now or never.

"What is it you're avoiding, Ash?"

Ash turned around and Draven saw his head hang. "My friend, Quinn. I need to talk with her, but I'm not sure how it's going to turn out, so I've been avoiding it. It's dumb, I know."

"No, it's not dumb," Draven said. "Difficult words aren't always easy to dish out, especially to those we care about, even more so when it's the opposite gender." Ash turned his head and Draven winked at him. "I may be able to use your help anyway."

"Really?" Ash asked him. Draven could tell that he'd piqued the boy's interest.

"Yeah. You're probably not going to like what I say next though."

"Only one way to find out," Ash said.

Draven broke the truth to him, "I don't think the Guardians are going to act in time to save the Forbidden from getting their souls drained. I have friends, and people I care about there. Most of which have never been involved in hurting anyone. Not to mention the innocent children that you spoke about from your vision." He saw Ash nod his head, saying nothing, so he continued.

"I've waited long enough for the Guardians to come to a decision, but I will wait no longer. I'm going to stop Aros myself. If you'd like to accompany me, I'd gladly have you join. Two strong mages are better than one. Yes, you're a very strong mage, especially to be so young." Now he was going to pile on the compliments. "Your lightning magic is more powerful than any other elemental wielding I've seen. Your hand-to-hand combat is nearly unrivaled. Of course, I've watched that Kane kid spar as well, and he is extremely gifted."

"Don't let him hear you say that," Ash joked. "His head may explode from the ego boost."

Draven chuckled even though he was in no laughing mood, "So, what do you say?"

Ash contemplated the proposition, "I'm in."

Quinn was so used to talking to Ash nearly every day that it felt odd to not have done so in the past few days. She could tell that he was avoiding her and she understood why, but all she wanted was to apologize and make things right if she could. It seemed like he always had someone around him and when she would begin walking in his direction, he would suddenly disappear in a crowd or around the corner of a building. She was resolving herself to sneak up on him if that's what it came to.

There was a knot in her stomach that hadn't gone away since the night she accidentally rejected him. All she wanted to do was be with Ash and now felt that she'd ruined her chances, seeing as he wouldn't even talk to her. Her mom wouldn't stop pestering her, trying to get her to open up about what was bothering her, but Quinn was too embarrassed to tell even her mother.

There was an audible clatter crashing around in Ash's home

as Quinn knocked on the door. A disheveled-looking Rick answered the door, dark shadows under his eyes. He looked rough. "Hey, Quinn. How are ya?" He asked her.

"I'm doing okay," she said. "How are you? I mean you look—"

"Awful? Yeah, I've been learning as much as I can about Asmaria. I'm hoping if I learn everything there is to know, the Guardians will allow me more freedom around here. Don't get me wrong, I'm grateful that they're letting me stay with Ash and work at the Café. I just want to do more. I spent so much of my life just sitting around, not contributing. I want to start over here, and if I show them I'm dedicated to being as Asmarian as possible, then hopefully they'll allow me to be more helpful."

"Well, I hope that works out for you. If there's anything I can do to help, just let me know," she told him, looking past him to see an empty house except for the books strewn all over the place. "Have you seen Ash?"

A knowing look crossed his face, "Ah, yeah. He's been leaving super early the past few days. Listen, I know things are sort of weird between the two of you right now, and I'd like to give you a little advice, if I may."

The horror she felt at knowing Ash had told him what happened between them was astronomical. All she could do was nod her head and he continued. "Ash has always been very determined. He may seem down for now, but he won't stay down for long. Just give him a little time and space and he'll come around eventually." Rick offered her a smile and she returned it.

"Thanks," she said. "I better be going. I should probably get some training done." She accepted Rick's advice, but heeding it was a different story. Quinn hiked to the training field where she hoped to find Ash. She scanned the area and saw him leaving with Draven so she jogged to catch up.

"Ash!" She shouted to get his attention. He said something to Draven who nodded and continued on the path that led into the jungle. The look on Ash's face made Quinn second guess herself, but she was determined to iron out all their issues right then. She tried a smile as she said, "I've been looking everywhere for you."

His expression was blank, unreadable, "I didn't want to be found."

"Yeah, I can tell. Look, about the other night, I—" Ash held up his hand and said, "Stop. We're going to have to finish this conversation another time." And then he turned his back to her.

Her face was red with anger now, "Hey!" He turned back to face her, "This is important. We need to talk about it."

"You're right," he said with a sad smile. "It is important, but right now there are more important things that I need to do."

"Like what?" She asked.

"Draven and I are going to save the people of the Forbidden."

Her eyes widened, "What? The Guardians haven't given any orders yet."

He turned back around, walked away, and said over his shoulder, "That's the issue. They're wasting too much time. We may already be too late, but if we can get there in time, Draven and I can do enough to keep those people from being drained."

Quinn couldn't believe he'd be so reckless. She jogged up and grabbed his wrist, yanking him back around to face her. His eyebrows knit together and she almost let go, worried that she was messing up again, but decided to hold fast. "You're being an idiot. How do you know you'll be able to stop Aros?"

He smiled, but it didn't seem like a happy smile, "Yeah, you're right. I *am* an idiot." Then he yanked his wrist free and walked toward the jungle. Quinn let him go this time, running toward the Guild building with tears sliding down her cheeks. She had to warn the Guardians and hoped they'd be able to stop them before they got themselves killed.

Ash found Draven on the southern shore of the island, loading his boat up and beginning to push it into the water. His temper returned to a normal level as he calmed down on the walk through the jungle. He was seeing why Draven was getting so upset. Everyone was taking their time to come up with a decision as to whether or not they would save the Forbidden from certain death. Even Quinn who was one of the smartest people he knew. Was he mad at her though? He wasn't sure; it could have been his fear of confronting her about the rejection that caused his anger. One thing he was sure of at this particular moment, was that there were innocent people that needed his help.

"So, what's the plan?" He asked Draven over the sound of waves crashing against the beach. This one wasn't nearly as pretty as the one on the North Shore.

"Surprise attack. We'll have to cut the motor as we get closer to the island. Climb up the rocks and attack Aros and Augustus together. You don't have a problem with fighting your father, right?" One of Draven's eyebrows was cocked up his forehead.

Ash almost laughed, "Are you kidding? After everything he's done? Killing my mother and abandoning me. Torturing my adoptive father, Rick. Kidnapping me last year and letting that demon possess me which got Ember, our last Guardian of Fire killed, and then nearly destroyed the Great Tree. Yeah, I have no problem taking that bastard down."

Draven held up his hands in defense, "Okay, sorry. I was just checking." And then his gaze went behind Ash. He said, "We'd better get going."

Ash turned around and saw several mages flying over the treetops toward them. He recognized them as Kane, Quinn, the three Guardians, and Kolin who was another wind mage. The three wind mages among them carried the others with strong gusts and only Kane seemed to not be having difficulty with the task. Ash gave credit to the Atlantean rings on his fingers. He looked to Draven as they landed in the sand, "Let me talk to them. Go ahead and take off, I'll catch up." When the guy gave him a questioning look, he just said, "Trust me." And then he was zooming away as fast as his boat would take him.

"Stop him," Avani told the water mages, but Ash couldn't allow that. He pulled at the energy that was humming on his skin, his palms erupting with crackling, purple lightning. Leena and Quinn stopped in their tracks.

"Ash, what do you think you're doing?" Bora questioned. Ash kept his eyes moving around the group; he knew who the *real* threats were.

"I'm doing what's necessary. I'm doing what you all are too scared to do. I'm helping my friend save his people." Avani and Kane were spreading out on either side of Ash, just as he figured they would.

"If you had just given us a little more time—" Avani began, but Ash interrupted. "Time is not a luxury we have! I saw them die! And I have continued to see them die nearly every night since then!" Ash could swear their faces were showing pity toward him. "You have to see that I'm right. Please just call the dragons and come with us before we're too late!" He was pleading with them now.

"I'm sorry to do this, Ash," Avani said, and then told the others, "Take him." The group began to close in on him, but he refused to be taken prisoner again. He pulled at more of the energy flowing through him. Lightning began swirling around his entire body and then the range of his power increased. He felt the ground beneath him begin to shift and he moved before it could swallow him up. He ran straight at Kane, thinking that he'd be more likely to forgive him than the others if they got hurt. Kane was still too fast though; he swung his fist at him from ten feet away. Ash's entire body was slammed from the side with an invisible force of wind that sent him sailing through the air above the sea. He could see it already curling up to snatch him as his lightning dissipated, one of the water mages bending it to their will.

Raimir! He called out with his mind. In a flash, the sky split, and lightning struck near the sandy beach. Raimir soared in with a screech, buzzing over the tops of the other mage's heads, causing them to dive onto the ground. He flew in and caught Ash with his strong talons and then tossed the boy in the air where he landed securely onto the bird's back.

You called? Raimir asked.

Ash wiped the sweat from his brow, looking back to see the island disappearing. *Thanks. Let's go save some people.*

As you wish, my friend.

Within a couple of minutes they had caught up with Draven. Ash saw the utter shock on his face as they flew in a wide circle around him, and Ash couldn't help but grin. They flew in close and the boat slowed down. "So that's what you meant by catch up, huh?" Draven yelled.

"Yep! I guess we'll just follow you from here. How fast can that thing go?"

"Probably not as fast as your ride!"

Ash chuckled, "Probably not."

The Might of an Atlantean

The sea was every Atlantean's true home. It is said that they are descendants of Poseidon himself. They couldn't exactly control the water, however, it would bend to their will and it's where they thrived. Thaoc followed his King through the salty waters. Holding his breath for hours on end was just as easy as breathing. The multitude propelled under the surface of the water at substantial speeds. The currents were reacting to the people's will as if the Atlanteans had never left the sea. The agriculture experts, the young, and the elderly would arrive by boat a time later.

Thaoc saw that King Gabriel was slowing down; he held his fist up for those behind to see and the signal was passed along through the ranks. They floated underwater and Thaoc heard the King's voice in his head—another ability of his people— saying "Asmaria is only a minute away. The waters will try to repel us, but we must break through. Don't attack unless your life is in danger, and even then, try to mitigate damage to our future allies. Spread the message among the soldiers." Thaoc telepathically relayed the King's order.

The sea floor had been too far down to see for such a long time, but now it was coming back to Thaoc's vision as they approached the island. They all were hit with a force that would have kept a normal person from passing, but they were not normal. With a mighty push of their combined wills, the Atlanteans burst through the current that was trying to push them away. Almost instantly, they were storming the beach and water mages were upon them. However, it was only two. The two mages looked petrified at first.

The King raised his hands, "Asmarians, we do not wish you or your island any harm. We are here to aid you in the war against the demon, Aros." The water mages looked confused, and then he saw the fear in their eyes as he stomped forward. Ocean water dripped from his curly beard and hair as he stood next to Gabriel. Their eyes widened at the sight of Thaoc; the sheer magnitude of the man would leave many of his foes paralyzed.

To set them at ease he knelt and laid his hammer beside him, "My friends, you needn't fear us. We are from Atlantis. Those kids, Ash and his friends, will vouch for us."

The two mages—who couldn't be older than 25—shared a look. One of them gulped and said, "Actually, the Guardians—our leaders—are right down there." He pointed down the beach and Thaoc followed his gesture where he could make out a group of people. They looked like specks from so far away.

King Gabriel said, "It would appear that time is of the essence. Would one of you be so kind as to escort us to the Guardians?"

Avani was beside himself; he couldn't believe that Ash could be such a moron. He didn't know what to think about Draven. He honestly believed the boy had good intentions, but he was so rash and too quick to act, however, he didn't think it would come to this. They didn't have time to assemble the Guild or anything, and now their hands were being forced to either go back up the boys or stay in Asmaria and leave them to whatever fate awaits.

The Guardian was tired. Not in the sense that he wanted to lay down and take a nap, but rather he was weary of everything that had occurred over the past year. He almost wanted to step down as Guardian, but knew that would leave his comrades to replace him with someone who could be as bad as Ember. They still hadn't found a new Guardian of Fire yet. After what happened with Ember they were trying to decide how to go about vetting and choosing the next one.

"I can't believe this," he scoffed. "What are we going to do now?" He was pacing up and down the beach.

"You're going to walk a trench into the beach if you don't calm down," Bora told him.

"Calm down?" He exclaimed, "How am I supposed to be calm now? That kid is going to get himself killed!" He heard a gasp come from Quinn and saw her cover her mouth.

"Is that—" Kane began, and then, "it is! The Atlanteans!" He began waving and took off in a jog. Avani spun around and saw a huge group of people heading their way. They looked like people who belonged to the sea. He and the other Guardians began making their way to them as Kane greeted who appeared to be their King.

"Hello," the King said. "I am Gabriel, King of Atlantis." Avani couldn't hide the shock. His eyes grew wide and his jaw slackened. He looked at Kane who was grinning like crazy. Avani could see the resemblance between the man and their stone statue back in the Capital. He even had a trident; it was magnificent.

The Guardians took turns introducing themselves and then Bora said, "I think I speak for the rest of my comrades here when I say I want to know your whole story, however, we find ourselves in a bit of a crisis right now."

"Is that so?" Gabriel asked. "Perhaps we may be of service. What has happened?"

"I'm sure you have heard all about the demon, Aros," Avani said. "That boy has run off to fight him all alone."

"Well," Bora started, "not entirely alone. He has another with him, a boy named Draven who betrayed the Forbidden. Gethin granted him some abilities, but we still feel that they've gone off to fight a losing battle. It would seem that our battle planning was not moving along hastily enough for the two boys to wait."

"My King," Leena said. "I know you all have only just arrived, but is there anything you can do to help us?"

Gabriel chuckled and tossed his crown onto the sand, "Please, just call me Gabriel. I have a feeling we're going to be here for a while, and if that's the case, you all are in charge, not me. My forces will do as you say." The soldiers behind him slapped their closed fists on their chests, the sound echoing around the beach.

"That's great," Bora said. "We didn't have time to gather the rest of our Guild before Ash and Draven took off. We also don't know where they're headed. None of us have been to the island where Aros is."

"That shouldn't be a problem," the largest man Avani had ever seen said, emerging from behind Gabriel, although it's not as if he could have been hidden by any of the others. He walked to the water and placed the palm of his hand on it, closing his eyes. After a few seconds, he looked up and said, "It's faint, but I can feel him."

"How do you know it's him?" Avani asked, mesmerized by

the powers of the man and his size.

"The signature he's leaving in the water is the only one that feels dark. I don't feel Ash though, are you positive they're together?"

"Ash is on a giant bird," Kane told him. "That's another long story. We'll have to fill you in later. It's probably better if Ash tells you himself, so how about we get to saving my best friend?" Kane held his hands out questioningly.

"With the signature being as faint as it is," the giant said, "we need to leave immediately."

"Then leave we shall," Gabriel said and then to the Guardians. "As long as that's okay with you, of course." The Guardians looked between one another, nodding.

Bora said, "Let's go. Any idea how we all will get there? Our magic will only take us so far."

Gabriel smiled, "We have that covered as well. Thaoc," he said, turning to the giant, "it's best if we don't take everyone. Grab around 20 of your best men and we will set out." Avani saw the giant pound his chest with a fist and walk into the crowd of people, issuing orders.

"Quinn," Leena called the girl over, "I need you to stay." She began to protest, but Leena continued, "We know how close you and Ash are. You're too emotionally invested and may be a liability. Plus, I need you to do something else for me."

Her eyes went down, "What can I do?"

"I'm leaving you in charge of these other Atlanteans. Take them to the Guild building and wait for our return. Have water and rations brought to them, I'm sure they're tired from their journey." Quinn nodded and backed away, sitting on a large rock. Avani almost felt bad for her.

"What about me?" Kane asked.

Avani leaned in, "You're coming with us. When we arrive, I want you to hang back momentarily and wait. Stay hidden and wait exactly three minutes, then I want you coming in with everything you've got."

"You got it," the boy said.

"Now then," Gabriel's voice boomed out. "I've got one more question for Kane." The boy turned toward him. "Where is my daughter?" His face darkened and Kane looked like he was going to be sick.

"If you're wondering if she's okay," Kane said, "she is. Right now, she's most likely hanging out on our training field. She spends a lot of time there. Her skills with daggers are almost as good as with the chakram now."

Gabriel's eyes narrowed, but he said, "Very well. I will see her after this." The man waded into the water and yelled, "Come! Let us go aid the lightning wielder!" Avani watched the other Atlanteans jump into the water and he followed, as did his comrades. Atlanteans were grasping their wrists and dragging them into the water. As an earth mage, Avani wasn't too fond of swimming but knew that the ground was beneath the water if he ever needed it. Being dragged under was different though, and he felt his pace quicken. Especially when he noticed the hand that was bigger than his head grabbing his forearm. He looked into the eyes of Thaoc, the colossus, and the man smiled.

Avani tried calming down as his head dipped below the surface of the water, and then he heard a voice in his head. *Don't worry, you'll be fine,* Thaoc told him. These Atlanteans were wrapped in all kinds of mystery. Then Thaoc blew bubbles into Avani's face and when he stopped there was an air pocket covering his nose and mouth and he could breathe again. He looked around and saw the same happening to the others.

Ready? The voice invaded his mind again and he nodded. Suddenly they were blasting through the water at a breakneck speed. The trip was already exhilarating. Avani didn't know what sort of magic this was, and had they not been on their way to possibly die, he would have been loving the experience.

Corruptor of Souls

Shortly after the medley group of warriors left to help Ash and Draven, more of the Atlanteans arrived. Quinn escorted them all back to the Guild building as she was instructed and ran into Kailani along the way. Several other teenage girls greeted her, nearly tackling the girl to the ground with fierce hugs. When she broke away from them, she asked Quinn what was going on and she explained what happened with Ash. She told her of the arrival of the Atlanteans and how she was ordered to bring them back here and await further instruction upon the Guardian's return.

"How did my father seem?" Kailani asked.

Quinn shrugged, "I couldn't tell how upset he was, but he wasn't happy about you leaving Atlantis so abruptly."

Kailani looked down at her feet, "I'm sure it's going to be a lovely conversation when he gets back here."

"I'm just hoping they all return in one piece." Quinn wasn't trying to dampen the mood any more than it already was, but she was worried. Worried that the cavalry wouldn't arrive in time. Worried that Ash would be killed before they were able to mend their relationship, friendship, or whatever they were to each other. Worried about the safety of the Guardians and the Atlanteans. She wasn't sure she would have made much of a difference, but she desperately wished she would have been able to go along and help. At least that way she wouldn't have to deal with not knowing. Not knowing what was happening was torture.

The Atlanteans barely fit in the Guild building; the rows of seats were full and more people were sitting down on the main floor. It took Quinn several tries—and the help of Kailani—to hush the chatter, and then told them to sit tight and be patient for their King's return. The children were becoming restless so she found some toys for them to pass the time with. She didn't know how much of the noise and not knowing what was happening out there she could take.

The wind rushed around Ash's body as Raimir blasted higher into the sky. Ash could see the island in the distance but couldn't make out any details of it yet. Draven was directly below them in the boat. Ash's stomach was left behind in the sky as Raimir abruptly plummeted toward the ocean. He gripped the bird's feathers with white knuckles and his feet lost their hold on the beast's body. He almost fell off but then Raimir leveled out and the acceleration slowed.

"What was that for?" Ash yelled.

That island is covered with people already. They could have seen us, and based on the sinister feeling emanating from that place, I doubt we'd want to be spotted too soon. I'm going to leave you with the other boy now to avoid being discovered. By the way, I think this is a dumb idea. Call me when you need me.

You didn't say if *I* need you, Ash told him, ignoring the comment about it being a dumb idea.

You are correct, Raimir responded. He then swooped over the boat, flipping and depositing Ash into it roughly. The creature then rocketed into the sky and disappeared with a crack of lightning. Ash hoped it was high enough in the atmosphere to go unnoticed. They were a couple hundred yards away from the island and Ash could now see the cave that Draven mentioned.

"Here," Draven handed him a boat paddle. "Too bad you're not a water mage." And then he killed the engine so they could sneak up to the rocks. The two began paddling as quietly as they could, but fervently.

Ash's neck was slick with sweat by the time they made it to the rocks surrounding the island. The crashing waves were loud so he figured they would be safe from discovery. Draven tossed a small anchor overboard and then they hopped out onto the rocks. They rested for only a minute or two and then began ascending the sides of the island. The top of the island was roughly forty feet high and they would have to scale steep boulders to reach it.

When they reached the top, they peered just over the edge, allowing only their eyes and above to be visible. Augustus had his back to them and the obelisk stood erect just a few feet away. The man was talking to the crowd of the Forbidden and Ash heard, "—and that is why your sacrifice here today will go down in the history books. You will not be forgotten." He continued but Ash got distracted; he was scanning the faces of the other Forbidden members.

Some of them had no expression whatsoever. Others had tears already streaking down their faces. More than he liked to admit seemed almost happy about giving their lives up. He wondered how many would try attacking them if the fight went on too long. He hoped they would be able to save them all now that he was seeing them this close. Seeing their faces made them seem more human than he previously thought of them. In none of his nightmares had he seen this angle, although the familiarity of it was beginning to scare him.

Ash looked over at Draven, his unlikely comrade, and he nodded. They pulled themselves up together and he heard gasps as the Forbidden took notice. Augustus spun around, a wry smile prying his lips apart. His black eyes were darker than night. Ash knew that meant the demon was inside him. "Welcome," he said to the boys in that rough, possessed voice. "We've been waiting so patiently for you to arrive." And then his grin grew wider.

Draven said, "Let them go, Augustus. We won't let you kill all my people."

"Let me?" He retorted, "Who are you to "let" me do anything? I am the vessel of the Demon King, his closest advisor, his sage of darkness! You two are nothing to me!" With each proclamation he took a step closer, and Ash would not allow him to take another.

He felt the lightning humming around his body. He opened his hand, pulling at the bow with his mind. It appeared in his hand with a snap. "Oh, new toys? Come on then?" Augustus taunted, waving them forward in a "come here" motion. Ash could see shadows creeping away from Draven. He reached for the bowstring and pulled it back. An arrow of lightning appeared, crackling with anticipation to be loosed.

Draven roared and thrust his hands out; the shadows at his feet exploded to life and raced toward the man like daggers. Ash let his arrow fly. The two forces were on course to collide at the same time, but at the last second a massive hand of darkness appeared from nowhere and swatted them away. Ash immediately nocked another electrifying arrow and let it fly.

He and Draven were attacking simultaneously, but each of their blows was swatted aside by their opponent, almost effortlessly. Ash could feel his frustration building. He put the bow away and the mark reappeared on his arm.

Lifting his hands, Ash began blasting bolt after bolt of purple lightning at his father in a deadly barrage, but none of them landed. The man was laughing as he diverted each of their attacks away from him. He was beginning to regret coming with Draven alone, wishing they had more backup. The boys were becoming exhausted; they both stopped their attacks for a moment to catch their breath. Augustus said, "Getting tired, are we? I haven't even *started* yet. Want to see something magnificent?" He began to swirl his hands around each other, a small ball of shadow forming and slowly growing larger. "It's amazing, the power that one demon can give you. Of course, he is the most powerful one to have ever lived, but still. Even in his weakened state, Lord Aros can lend me more than enough power to smite the two of you, even with Draven's little upgrade."

When the sphere of black was about the size of a basketball, he split it in two and threw both parts onto the ground where they writhed. He clapped his hands together and uttered, "Rise." The black spheres began to shift and take on a different shape entirely. They grew to over six feet tall, arms and legs protruding from the center mass, a head popping out. They looked as if they were someone's shadow, except more menacing. They began stomping their way toward the duo. Augustus was already turned back, facing the crowd of Forbidden who hadn't moved. Then Ash noticed why; they were strapped down by shackles made of shadow.

"We have to stop him!" Draven shouted as Augustus started

chanting something in a different language. Ash retrieved his bow again and gave it everything he had, loosing arrow after arrow at the stalking shadows. Chunks of the one in front of him were being blasted apart, but the creature kept coming. Draven tripped his target with tendrils of black and then ripped the thing in two, causing it to vanish. Then he made a slicing motion and the head of the shadow stalking toward Ash separated from its body, causing it to vanish as well. They charged toward Augustus together.

Suddenly, two tentacles of darkness sprang from the ground and wrapped around their throats. They clawed at the tendrils but they wouldn't budge. Ash shot bolts of lightning at Augustus, but even with his back turned, shadows slapped the bolts away. Draven's shadow magic was useless as well. Augustus hadn't even broken focus. Ash wondered if they had underestimated him *that* badly. Augustus stopped chanting, and the people of the Forbidden began to rise from the ground. *Oh no,* Ash thought. This was his vision, the recurring nightmare. Ash stopped attacking; it was pointless and he could feel his energy waning.

Their bodies curved backward and their mouths were agape as Aros filtered out of his vessel's body. The gaping mouths glowed blindingly white, and then their souls began to siphon out. Streaks of the brightest white Ash had ever seen issued from every person as if the souls were made from clouds of light. The demon absorbed each one of them, his shadowy body growing from its infantile shape to that of a grown man, the same as the first time Ash saw him. He flexed his fingers as the Forbidden member's bodies dropped to the ground, lifeless. It all happened so fast and it was so horrifying that Ash had completely forgotten to reach out to Raimir.

"Now then," Aros' soothing voice said as he turned to face the boys. Ash could see his glowing yellow eyes. "For the final steps of the ritual. Augustus, the stone." He held out his hand and Augustus pulled something from his pocket. Ash tried squirming free but it was futile. Aros placed a small stone into a triangular slot on the obelisk. The carvings glowed blue and Ash could feel a dark energy hum within the obelisk.

Draven was dropped down to his hands and knees. He tried to wield shadows, but he was quickly overpowered by Aros. "The blood of the traitor," Aros said as he dragged the boy toward the obelisk. "The conclusive element to bringing my body back."

"You knew? This whole time?" Draven asked.

Aros chuckled, "Of course I knew." The demon held Draven up against the obelisk. Ash could see his chest rising and falling rapidly. He struggled against the tendril of darkness that was still wrapped around his throat, but it wouldn't give. Then horror struck him like a bolt of lightning as one of Aros' arms turned into a giant blade of obsidian. He plunged it deep into Draven's stomach, an evil grin on his face. Draven's mouth was agape, shock overtaking the pain he was probably feeling. Blood trickled down the surface of the obelisk. Aros released Draven and his body slumped to the ground.

Ash tried to scream, but the constriction on his throat wouldn't allow it. He yanked with all his might, trying to get free of the hold Augustus had on him. He could feel the dark vines getting weaker but his energy faded first. He could feel his eyes burning from the salty tears building.

A sinister, maniacal laugh issued from Aros as his body began to change. Flesh started growing at his feet and continued upward. It went on until he had a physical body of his own. A pair of brown pants covered his lower half, but the top portion was shirtless. The demon's new body was almost grey and had black veins spiderwebbing everywhere. His feet were bare and his toenails were far too long. The nails of his fingers matched, each one coming to a sharp point. Ash could see that the rest of his body was toned to perfection. He looked like someone who worked out for three hours a day.

Ash noticed his eyes had changed from yellow to white, the irises and all. Aros smiled widely and Ash wanted to throw up. His teeth were mostly perfect, but his gums looked black. The hair on his head was blacker than anything Ash had ever seen. It looked like dark smoke was wafting off him as he moved about. Footprints were being burned into the ground as he stepped closer to Ash. The grass beneath burned to a crisp.

The grip on Ash was faltering; he knew that Augustus's shadow-wielding would be lessened when Aros wasn't occupying his body. He only had one shot to escape and his timing had to be perfect. Aros had to be less than ten feet away now, his disgusting smile growing wider with each step. "All this would have been easier if you Asmarians would have just let that Tree die. But no, you had to save it. Well now, there will be no saving your world." Aros chuckled, "I will destroy…everything."

Now. Ash gave in to the pull of energy and yanked his arm free as lightning arced all around him. He dragged in a deep breath of fresh air, "RAIMIR!" He screamed, feeling the force of it tearing at his throat. Aros' foot connected with his chest. It was so fast that Ash hadn't seen it coming. He flew backward, flipping over and over. When his body stopped rolling he was hanging halfway off the edge of the island cliffs. He hadn't blacked out, which surprised him considering the amount of pain he was now feeling. His body was rife with agony, and he didn't want to know how many bones were broken. Then lightning cracked open the sky and he heard the familiar screech of Raimir.

He saw the bird fly over the island, lightning arcing around his wings as he circled. *Why didn't you call sooner?* He grumbled.

All Ash could think was, *I'm sorry.*

He was able to prop himself on his elbows, thankful that his arms weren't too damaged from the blow. The ache in his ribs told him that they took the brunt of the damage. His legs felt like they had been filled with steel as he dragged himself a few feet from the edge of the cliff.

He watched Raimir dive down, hovering over their enemies. The bird flapped his wings once and a powerful strike of lightning rained down. Aros lifted one hand and a shield of darkness covered them, absorbing the blast. Raimir landed and Ash knew that was a mistake. Vines of darkness shot from the ground and wrapped around his feet. He bent his legs and tried to jump and he made it several feet off the ground, flapping his wings, but then the vines yanked him back down.

As he was being held captive, Ash saw Augustus' hand erupt in flame. He reared his arm back and hurled a blast of fire at Raimir. The creature saw it coming and was able to dodge it, despite the hold that the shadowy tentacles had on him. His father was preparing to send another pillar of flame at his companion, but Ash mustered enough strength to let loose the smallest bolt of lightning. It landed true in the center of the man's back, causing him to fall forward. He smacked his head on the obelisk and was rendered unconscious.

Okay, now it's just down to Aros, Ash thought.

Thank you, my friend. Now let's take down this beast, once and for all.

I'd love to help, but I think I'm spent, Ash guiltily responded.

Raimir glanced over at him, still trying to get away from the black vines. *You just stay there then. I'll handle this.*

More shadows curled around his legs and a cry of desperation escaped his beak. Ash forced himself to his feet, pain shot through his ankle but he didn't think it was broken. He hobbled forward, taking in shallow, painful breaths. Ash hobbled over to Draven; he may not have the energy to wield any more lightning, but he had to check on him. Ash heard Aros laughing as he made his way to the young man.

Raimir's voice boomed in Ash's mind, *You must free me from these shadows! I can't get them to budge!*

With Aros' attention fully on Raimir and Augustus temporarily incapacitated, Ash pulled his bow back out. That effort alone caused his vision to blur, but his aim was still true. He was able to create two arrows simultaneously. He shot them at Raimir, each one hitting the base of the shadow curling up the bird's body. The vines snapped and he shot up into the air. Aros whirled around, seething.

Ash put his bow back into place and conjured blades of lightning in his hands. His body swayed, threatening to topple over at any moment. He couldn't move much, but he didn't need to when the enemy was charging at him. Aros got within range. Ash swung but the demon dodged him easily, his movements had slowed. His hands gripped one of Ash's arms; his touch felt like dry ice, both burning and freezing at the same time. He wrenched the boy's arm behind his back and pushed him to the ground, placing a knee in his back. Ash could hear him snickering as he pushed the arm further up, his shoulder crackling and popping as the tendons snapped. The demon's body was flung off him as his cries of pain rang out across the island.

Ash was able to roll over, his arm flopping around uselessly. He laid on his back after Raimir had smacked the demon with a talon. A wound opened up on Aros' forehead, bleeding slightly with a black goo. His skin knit itself back together quickly, much to Ash's horror. The ichor retreated back into the laceration. Aros recovered to his feet and in one outstretched hand, a black whip appeared. He snapped it at the giant bird, the end of it wrapping around one of his legs.

He tried feebly to pull away but Aros was overpowering him. Aros stretched out his other hand and a scythe issued from the ground. Its obsidian blade gleamed in the sun. With a grunt, Aros yanked on the whip and then jumped. The demon leaped at least fifteen feet from the ground, swinging the scythe. One of Raimir's wings was severed and the creature fell. Screeching cries of pain echoed around and then the voice filled Ash's head.

I... I... must go back to my realm before I die. I'm... sorry. And then the familiar crack of lightning sounded, Raimir vanishing from the island. The wing that had been severed turned to dust as the giant falcon vanished.

Aros sauntered over, laughing gleefully, "All of this could have been avoided had you just given yourself over to me willingly." He bent down and got within inches of Ash's face, a putrid smell filled his nostrils. "You are much more stubborn than your father. All I had to do was offer him the one thing he wanted most and he broke," Aros snapped his fingers, "just like that. Promise him the safety of his family and he turns into my puppet."

What was he talking about? "What do you mean?"

He chuckled, "Your daddy didn't tell you? No, of course he didn't. Well, it doesn't matter if you know now or not. In exchange for joining my side, I promised your father that when I burn this world down and create it anew, I'd revive your dear mommy and keep you safe. The three of you would be the first humans in the new world I create. Of course, I do not have the power to revive anyone from the dead. Not as they once were; I could have brought back her body to life, but it would have been an empty, soulless shell. Now, however, I'm thinking I'll kill you here and then your father. Once I'm done using him of course. Simply because you've been such a thorn in my side."

Aros stood up, stretching his arms. Ash felt a rush of braveness. What did it matter now that he was about to die anyway? "You're going to pay for what you've done here today."

The demon chuckled, "Oh, am I? And who is going to make me pay?"

"Me," Ash said.

He laughed boisterously, "Do you not realize who I am, boy? I am the Merchant of Darkness, Corruptor of Souls, Master of the Damned! Do you *honestly* believe you can defeat me? You, and what army?"

Thaoc and the other Atlanteans dove down deeper and then arced back up as they approached the island. They used all their gained momentum to blast out of the water and easily launched to the top, landing lightly. The scene displayed before him made Thaoc's stomach turn. He'd seen much death in his time, but the frail bodies of women and children strewn about made him sick. On the opposite side of the small island stood a creature with black, smoke-like wisps slipping off its skin. A tall scythe in one hand.

"That's him," Avani uttered. "The demon, Aros. Except now he has a body. That looks like Ash he's standing over." Without waiting for anyone else, the Guardian began sprinting in their direction. Everyone followed. Thaoc was on his heels when the demon turned on them and swung the scythe horizontally through the air at them. A blade of shadow soared at Avani but Thaoc was able to jump in its path, absorbing it with the Hammer of Ogun. The dark energy didn't feel good in his hands; he immediately raised the hammer and swung it forcefully, sending the blast back at the demon.

Aros easily ducked the attack and an evil grin spread across his face. He yelled to them, "Here, play with my pets!" He struck the ground with the butt of his scythe; two large creatures crawled up the cliff behind him and he pointed at the cavalry, ordering, "Kill them." The two beasts charged.

Thaoc hadn't seen something so reviling in his time. Behind him, he heard Leena mutter, "Karnigrots." They were easily the size of a normal human, with furry bodies, sharp claws, and a scaly tail like that of a snake. The beasts bared their nasty fangs as they ran toward them. Avani tried to swallow them up by shifting the ground, but they were too nimble and moved around too quickly.

Within seconds the karnigrots were upon them; the Guardians jumped in front and, with their combined power, were able to slow the beasts down. Bora used gusts of wind to hinder their movements. Leena sent a vortex of currents around the two, causing them to fall end over end, suspended a few feet above the ground. Avani conjured spikes of death that pierced the beast's thick hide. The elements were released and the karnigrots slumped onto the ground, lifeless. Thaoc was impressed with the cohesion that the Guardians possessed.

Thaoc had been too surprised by the attack to pay attention to Aros, but it was now evident that the demon had moved during the attack. He was now standing next to the obelisk, a great shadowy tentacle protruded from his side and wrapped around the stone structure. His scythe had vanished and he held a limp body over his shoulder. Another body lay on the ground next to the base of the obelisk. "I hope you enjoy my parting gift," he said with a disgusting smile. Then he took a deep breath and blew out a cloud of black steam which passed over each of the deceased bodies. Black wings protruded from his back, unfolding as his shoulders bobbed with laughter.

"Stop him!" Avani shouted. The Atlanteans surged forward. The Asmarians sent a shockwave of their elemental magic at him, but they were too slow. Thaoc watched the magic soar past him as he lumbered forward; Aros bent his knees and then launched into the air. His wings sent him, the obelisk, and the body he took away. Avani shot spikes of rock at the demon, but he rose quickly and was out of range. The rocks tumbled into the surrounding waters without touching their target. Thaoc saw Kane about to pursue him, but Avani held his arm out to stop him, shaking his head. "Look," the Guardian said.

All around them, the bodies began to stir, safe for the one that had been near the obelisk. The previously dead beings were reanimated, shadow puppets with the orders to kill them. "This can't be real," Bora shuddered, her hands trembling.

"They wouldn't want themselves to be used like this," Gabriel told them all. "Do them the service of ending this abhorrent existence." He struck down one of them with his trident as it pierced the heart.

Thaoc was a General, but down to his roots, he was just a soldier. The acts they all committed for these people were not merciless, but merciful. Even with that knowledge, watching the bodies fall, and dropping many himself was sickening. Men, women, children, mostly innocent. But it had to be done. They weren't alive even now that they were reanimated. They were merely undead.

After it was over, Thaoc sat down on a rock, cleaning his hammer. The Asmarians huddled around Ash. Thaoc joined them to check on the boy. "How is he?"

"He's alive," Leena said. "But there's no telling what sort of internal damage has been done. He keeps fading in and out, but he won't speak." Thaoc looked at him, his arm bent at an odd angle. He looked like he was struggling to breathe and his eyes were red, his cheeks wet.

Avani was cradling the other boy in his arms, his head on the man's lap. "Just try to breathe. Slow, steady breaths," he heard him say as he turned his attention to them.

"I'm sorry," the boy uttered with gasping breaths. Blood trickled from his lips and covered his stomach.

"Shh," Avani told him. "Save your energy, don't talk. You're going to be fine. We'll get you back to Asmaria and you'll be good as new." However, as he said it, the boy pushed out a final breath and ceased all movement. Avani cursed under his breath as he laid Draven's head down on the ground and folded his eyelids down with a bloody hand.

Avani stood, wiping his hands. "Let's get the boys back home. Draven will get a proper Asmarian burial. He may have come to us from the enemy, but he died fighting to stop the Asmarian people's biggest threat."

"We're wasting time here then," Kane said. Ash's body rose from the ground. Kane carried him with wind over the edge of the island and lowered him into the boat they must have used to get there. The Asmarians clamored down into the boat with Ash and Draven, waiting for the Atlanteans to vacate the island. Gabriel motioned for them to follow and, with a running jump, dove headfirst into the sea.

Thaoc surfaced and watched as Avani spread his arms out in a T and then clapped his hands together. A force rang out and the waves crashed as the island folded in on itself, sinking into the sea and hiding away all the evil things that just occurred. As it disappeared, Leena began wielding the ocean water to send them back to Asmaria faster than the motor could have.

Thaoc heard the King's voice in his head as he addressed them all, *Our Asmarian friends need us now more than ever. We must show our support and help them in any way possible. We shall make a home for ourselves on Asmaria for as long as they'll have us. I know that what we had to do here today was difficult, and I don't take it lightly. I thank you all for your courage to do the right thing. Now, let us go be with the rest of our people.*

Subconscious Sanctum

The boy born in a lightning bolt who would either save this world or be its downfall. That was his alleged destiny, fate, or whatever they wanted to call it. Ash had originally thought that he would be the bring the end of the world by being Aros' vessel. Now, however, he was feeling like he could end the world as he knew it all on his own. First, he'd gotten captured by Augustus and taken to the Forbidden's lair. He'd allowed himself to become possessed by Aros, leading to the demon striking the Great Tree with a mixture of Ash's and his dark powers.

Ash was different from most of the other Asmarians. They wished to see him locked up for accusations of treason. All he wanted at the time was to be sent out in search of a cure for the Tree. He'd done that, of course, he wasn't alone in that venture. What had he accomplished on his own? Nothing that he could think of. No, there was always someone else there to help him. It was only his failures that he could take full credit for.

To be the world's savior was the destiny portrayed for him. However, all he'd ever done was fail and get those he cared about hurt. That must be his true fate, to fail, over and over again. The crushing weight of guilt kept him from talking or moving, and he wished it would end his breathing. He knew he was too stubborn to die from his penitence. Maybe if he retreated into himself he could disappear within the confines of his mind and forget about everything that happened.

Rick. Ember. Gethin. Draven. Raimir. The first one he'd nearly killed all because of his selfish desire to leave their home. The next one he'd murdered. Sure, it was Aros using his body, but had Ash not been so weak as to let himself be possessed, then Ember would still be alive. Gethin was almost destroyed because of the same reason. Had the Tree been killed, magic would have been destroyed as well and Aros would already be conquering the world.

Then there's Draven. Ash wasn't granted enough time with the guy to get to know him very well, or perhaps deep down he knew that those close to him ended up hurt or worse. Maybe his subconscious didn't want him to make a new friend who would inevitably meet their demise after being around him. He wasn't sure. Thinking of all the possibilities of what could have been shattered, Ash. Not only could Draven have been a close friend, but he would have been a valuable asset as well. He, like Ash, had been gifted magic that no one else in Asmaria could replicate. With more training, Ash knew he would have been a gifted warrior.

Raimir had quickly become one of Ash's closest allies. The beast was always but a thought away. Always there when Ash needed him, even if it was just to complain about his girl trouble. He didn't know if the bird was alive or not, but he hoped he was okay. Two dead allies in a single day was unbearable to even fathom.

All Ash had to do was stop him from going to that island. All he had to do was convince him to wait for the Guardians. It was so simple when he thought about it. He was—once again—thinking more of his problems, rather than using his brain to protect someone. He was so scared of facing Quinn again that he wasn't thinking clearly at the time.

From the moment he was rescued all semblance of time receded. Ash couldn't feel anything and his mind was dark, but he did have his thoughts. The darkest thoughts in the recesses of his mind were his only companions now. He was glad he couldn't feel anything physically after remembering how broken Aros left him. He remembered the Guardians showing up with others, although he couldn't tell who they were before he blacked out.

Voices from the outside world filtered in here and there, but he could only recognize his name through the jumble. "Wake up, Ash," they would say. But he refused. Nothing would pull him out of this chasm of darkness he now found himself in. Where he had retreated to, he knew that no one would be harmed because of him, and that was worth everything.

There was no way for him to tell how much time had passed. It felt like he was asleep the entire time, but he still felt aware of his thoughts. Now and then he would reach out with his mind, *Raimir,* he would whisper. Ash didn't know what kept causing him to reach out; maybe it was just him wanting to see if Raimir was alive, or perhaps it was his selfish desires hoping that he wasn't the cause of another comrade's death. There had yet to be any answer from his friend, so Ash still didn't know if he was alive or not.

The outside world moved on without him; he could hear it. Familiar voices were ubiquitous in his ears for the most part, although, most of the time Ash couldn't decipher the words being said. He could make assumptions, but could never be sure. That was the case until she spoke to him; he heard everything then.

"Ash, please," he heard the familiar voice plead. "Please wake up. You have to be okay." Quinn was begging him to come out of his stupor, but he wouldn't. She was safer this way. She was safer without the threat of his existence. All of his friends that he'd made in Asmaria would be better off without him. Rick would be safe. It would all be okay. Ash retreated deeper into his mind, the outside voices—including Quinn's—vanishing.

Weeks. Weeks gone by since Draven was killed and Ash was badly injured. Kane was infuriated. Part of his anger was directed at the Guardians, and part of it was aimed at himself. Ash had become his best friend and he never even realized what he was going through. After their return to Asmaria, Ash was taken to the hospital. Kane wouldn't leave his side and Quinn arrived shortly thereafter. He explained everything and she in turn told him that she believed it was her fault.

Quinn broke down, telling him about how Ash had tried kissing her and she rejected him. She didn't even understand why she'd done it, other than she was shocked and nervous. Kane had wrapped his arms around her until the sobs stopped. She couldn't blame herself. Kane blamed the teenage boy hormones that caused Ash to act so erratically. He didn't even care whose fault it was, he just wanted his brother-in-arms to wake back up.

No matter what they tried, Ash wouldn't open his eyes. His injuries were healing nicely as the heala being forced into him spread around and mended his body. Kane had tried to stir the boy but there was no reaction. Quinn tried to wake him and Kane thought that would work, but still, he slept hard.

Kane hardly ever left the hospital room as he was determined to be by his side when his best friend woke up. His worry over Ash's well-being was greater than the concern over his training standards faltering. He couldn't very well practice with weaponry, but the floor made a great place to do push-ups and other bodyweight exercises. Rick also came and went every day. As the days wore on, the man looked more dreadful.

"How is he today?" Rick would ask. Kane would merely shake his head with disappointment.

The Guardians came by for the first few days, but it had now been at least five weeks since Kane had seen them. His frustrations with them increased as it seemed they'd given up on Ash. He found himself surprised when Avani came by one day.

He told Kane, "I need you to come with me." Kane was about to protest, but the Guardian said, "It's non-negotiable. Come."

The urgency in his face got Kane to his feet and they left the hospital. "What's going on?" Kane asked as they walked at a brisk pace. Something critical was happening in the world.

"We've been working on something while Ash is recovering," Avani said. "The Atlanteans and Rick happen to be very good with technology. For the past few weeks, they've been working on a device that will allow us to keep tabs on things going on in the rest of the world. It's a mixture of old technology that we've kept in a warehouse for years and Atlantean runes. It would seem they have an answer for everything."

"I don't understand," Kane said.

"Without having any eyes and ears outside of Asmaria, we needed a way to know how strong Aros is becoming, or if he's doing anything nefarious. As expected, he's up to something, we just need to know what, and we can't afford to spread ourselves thin by having people running around spying on him."

Kane's concern was growing, "So, what of the technology you mentioned?"

"The device is working now, and Aros hasn't wasted any time in reaching his goal. He's building an army."

"You could have just told me this," Kane said. "Why drag me away from Ash to show me?"

"I need all of my best mages to know what we're up against. I need you to start preparing. Not just yourself, but others as well." Again, the distinct tone Avani was using gave Kane pause. He knew the Guardian to be stoic and unbothered, but now it was as if his voice was riddled with fear.

They entered a small building at the end of the street near where the Café sat. It didn't look special in any way, however, Kane's eyes met Kailani's and she had a look of alarm on her face. He'd come to know her very well and could tell when something was off with her. She'd come to visit him and Ash and told him about her father's reaction upon seeing her. She was worried he was going to disown her or something, but he simply wrapped his muscled arms around her in a warm embrace, telling her how much he missed her. Kane was glad Gabriel was such a kind and understanding man. He worried that he would be the target of his anger, but that had passed.

Kailani greeted them and followed the two of them inside. There were four massive screens in the room with several buttons and switches on a long panel before the screens. Rick stood there with a few Atlanteans he didn't recognize. The sides of the screens had glowing runes carved into them. It was like a computer; Kane had never seen one, but he'd read about them. On the screens were moving images that were so crystal clear Kane felt like he was in the scene playing out.

Rick saw the confused look on Kane's face as he started explaining, "There's a device called a camera which is how we can see the picture on the screen. It's a little rectangular box that can show us videos from the other side of the world. The small black thing she's holding is called a microphone. It allows us to hear what she's saying."

Funnily enough, Kane thought it sounded a bit like magic. "I have, of course, read of these things before. I just never thought it would be so realistic."

The woman stood on a street in front of a cemetery speaking directly to the camera, "—all 1500 graves at this cemetery were found empty over the weekend. It is uncharacteristic of grave robbers to take the bodies, especially at this magnitude. Authorities have also yet to figure out how the bodies were removed. The evidence left at the scene does not indicate that they were dug out." The camera panned over to the cemetery and Kane could see that the missing bodies seemed to have crawled out of their resting place of their own volition.

"How do we know this is Aros?" Kane asked those in the room.

One of the Atlanteans answered, "We've enchanted this computer with runes to only show signs of great evil. It doesn't matter where in the world it's located, as long as it is being televised in some way, we'll have access to it."

"Apart from the whole 'evil' thing, that's pretty cool," Kane said.

"Kane," Avani said, "I'm putting you in charge of training the wind mages. Bora will be there to help but to be honest, you've become more powerful than even her." When Kane smiled, Avani said, "Do not tell her I said that."

"You got it," Kane laughed. "What about the Atlanteans?"

"They will be given free rein of Asmaria and the surrounding waters as they see fit. We will develop training days where everyone will work together. It will be a combined effort of all our abilities."

Kane's brows knit together, "And what about Ash?"

"Seeing as Ash is comatose," Avani said, "we will just have to wait for him to wake. When, or if, he does, then we will have to have a long talk with him. I don't want him to be in trouble any more than you do, but given the circumstances, he will have to be punished. He disobeyed and attacked us and that, we cannot allow."

"Understood," Kane said. "So, what's our next move?"

"We want to begin training within the next few days. We've no idea the timeframe needed before Aros begins his next assault. We plan to keep tabs on his operations as best we can, but in the meantime, our forces need to be ready for anything."

Kane was determined to create the most deadly fighting force in all history. The Spartans he'd read about would look like children compared to the mages he would mold. His elite warriors of the wind would show no mercy to their enemies. If he wanted to bring this dream to fruition, he'd better get started. "Kailani, walk with me," Kane said. The air was cool on his skin when they exited the building. Kane wasn't sure if she would understand.

"I want you to know how much my time with you means to me," he told her. "I don't want it to end so soon, but I also want you to understand something. My main focus has to be this war. If I slack off in my duties now, we're doomed."

She laughed, "I understand, Kane. You're so caring, gentle, and kind. I never would have pegged you as being so fierce, and yet here we are." She took his hands in hers, stood on the tips of her toes, and planted a kiss on his cheek.

Kane's smile could have torn his face apart for how wide it was. "You're the best," he said, pulling her into his arms. What was he so worried about? Of course, she would understand. She was the coolest girl he'd ever met. Kane couldn't wait for the war to be over so that they could live out their days together.

This is much better, Ash thought. The lack of voices besides his own gave him a strong sense of peace and clarity. It could have been days, weeks, or months since someone tried to wake him and he wouldn't know the difference. He was living inside his head, filtering through his favorite memories and replaying them one by one. He purposely sped past the bad ones, the darkest days he'd lived. He didn't want to think about any of that.

Ash didn't want to see the bad things. He didn't want to live through the hell he'd already endured, nor see his mistakes again. Those were worse than the broken bones or any physical pain inflicted upon him. He wouldn't think about being abandoned as a baby, and would only think of Rick as he'd known him in recent months. The image of being stuck in that small, dingy apartment would be no good. The memory of his broken body was pushed from his mind as well as all the horrors in between.

He didn't want to see anything that would cause him more grief, more remorse. Any other boy of fourteen could never endure such things and continue. That's what Ash told himself anyway. That statement—whether it be fact or opinion—comforted him slightly. The darkness in his mind was a safety blanket from the evil world beyond.

For a brief moment, the outside world ceased to exist as Ash found solace within the rich tapestry of his memories. They were a labyrinth, a maze, a kaleidoscope of visions passing by him. When the scene found its way to show his friends, he paused there. Quinn's smiling face burned into his mental retinas. Kane's familiar white hair shone in the sun. That was almost enough to make him change his mind. Almost. Then it was like he could feel the soft downy feathers of Raimir's back as they flew above the ocean. The electrifying feeling that had coursed through him when the beast showed him how fast he could fly.

How long had it been since he reached out for the magnificent creature? Ash had no idea. It felt like mere minutes and several days had passed by simultaneously. Time was a fickle thing in the mind prison.

Raimir, he thought. He would try once more to reach his friend, *Raimir, are you there?*

I'm here, my friend.

Ash's eyes snapped open, the light of the real world instantly blinding him as reality rushed back into existence.

Epilogue

Many changes were taking place in the world as Ash lay in his slumber. Aros, now back to full strength, was gathering the forces that he would use for the final battle. Once his army was complete, Aros would have nothing left to do besides attempting to dominate the world. The demon king was confident that he would become the ruler of the planet, and enslave mankind. Aros' command over the dead and other disgusting creatures locked within the confines of the Earth would prove to be devastating in the coming war.

The Earth was molting as darkness crept into it caused by Aros. With the help of the Atlanteans, the leaders of Asmaria learned as much as they could about their enemy while their warriors prepared for battle. Normal humans with no magical ability were becoming uneasy; riots were popping up all over the world as Aros' influence took hold of them. Violent crime across all nations was at an all-time high. They would be at war with themselves before long, and the Guardians feared that it would be too late to recover if they didn't stop Aros soon.

Many beasts lay under the Earth's surface, that which hadn't been seen by any person alive. Aros is older than almost every living thing and his knowledge of evil beings was boundless.

The king of demons no longer had any use of his previous cohort, Augustus. Now that Aros had recovered his full body, he didn't have to possess someone to move away from the obelisk freely. Still, Aros kept the man around, bound with dark magic just in case he found a use for him before the war was over.

A team of Asmarians and Atlanteans alike was assembled to help train the non-magic people on their island. A lot of them were handy with weapons, however, they needed to become proficient before the war began. The world would need all the soldiers it could get its hands on if it was going to stop Aros.

The most peculiar of changes currently happening was that of the Great Tree. It, or She, was undergoing a transformation of Her own. The Great Tree was a fitting name, for the Tree was taller, wider, and had more branches than any other on Earth. The Asmarians had never realized the magnitude of it. Now, however, layer upon layer was being peeled away from the Tree. It was almost as if the hard exterior of the Tree was a cocoon of sorts.

One year later...

The lights of the hospital room blinded Ash immediately, forcing him to slam his eyelids shut. He took a few uncomfortable breaths and then began slowly pulling the tubes from his throat. The ragged breath that he drew burned his throat. His eyes crept open painstakingly slowly to allow them to adjust to the bright fluorescent lights. Most of Asmaria was lit by flaming torches, however, the hospital was almost identical to any Ash had seen on TV when he lived in the apartment with Rick.

Rick, Ash thought, *I wonder how worried he was about me.*

Beeping machines filled Ash's ears as he continued to rip wires off his body and attempted to get up. He slammed into the floor, his legs barely able to move. Panic was setting into Ash as he wondered how long he'd been lying in the hospital bed. He tried to prop himself up but his arms were too weak to hold his body off the floor. He just laid there, drool puddling under his cheek.

Finally, someone entered the room and helped him up. "Welcome back to the land of the living," the nurse said. "You've been out of commission for quite a while young man."

"Just how long have I been asleep?" he asked.

"I'd say it's been roughly a year now since they brought you in here."

A year? But how could that be? It seemed like just yesterday that he and Draven had run off to fight Aros and Augustus alone. The thought of Draven was like a stab to Ash's chest. Ash thought the lady was mistaken, but then, why would he be so weak if not for being bedridden for so long?

The Guardians were watching over Kane and how he was conducting training some of the wind mages. He had taken to teaching them like a fish to water. It was second nature to the boy. Avani was originally concerned that the young mage would falter and need more direction when it came to training others. Now though, he was confident that Kane was meant for this role.

It was important for the younger kids to be given duties to help keep them out of trouble and give them a sense of purpose. One of the common jobs for them was that of messenger. A young girl ran up to Avani and whispered something to him, and then turned and ran off. The other Guardians took note.

"What was that all about?" Bora asked.

Avani looked grim, "Ash is awake."

Raimir waited patiently for Ash to be ready to see him. The creature had seen much in his time. He'd fought many battles in various universes and had witnessed a plethora of death and destruction. However, he had never been hurt as badly as he was this last time by Aros. Raimir berated himself for allowing Ash to drag him along; he should have prevented him from going after the demon alone.

Underestimating the power of the demon king was a mistake that Raimir would never make again. There was something about the strength within Ash that had caused Raimir to throw caution to the wind and charge in without a good battle plan. It had been a long time since Ash had reached out to him, but Raimir knew that the boy was still alive; he could feel it. However, he had just fully recovered when Ash's voice filled his mind.

The connection they shared had been weak for so long that Raimir worried if Ash would ever wake from his slumber. He couldn't see directly into his mind, but he was intuitive enough to know what was happening usually. The beast was thrilled to know that his ally had awakened. He was eager to be by his side, to be back in the fight, but he had learned from the past and would not come until Ash asked for him. He assumed correctly that there were things Ash would need to sort out before Raimir joined him once again.

About the Author

DC Sumner goes by many titles. Some of them include Christian, husband, father, and now, writer. Mr. Sumner serves as a Unit Training Manager in the US Air Force and hopes to be a best-selling author one day.

Besides reading and writing, some of his hobbies are hanging out with his family, watching The Office on repeat, and practicing Brazilian Jiu-Jitsu. DC loves to make new friends and meet new people. One of his biggest hopes for this writing journey is to inspire others to follow their dreams.

You can connect with me on:

 https://dcsumner.com

 https://is.gd/qkC1u1

Also by DC Sumner

The Chronicles of Ash is an Urban Fantasy series that takes place on a mysterious island called Asmaria. On this island, some of the inhabitants are gifted with the ability to wield one of four elements: fire, water, wind, and earth.

Great book! Fun, imaginative, & exciting! —Stephanie, GoodReads.com

For a first-time author, I genuinely enjoyed this book. A little rushed in some spots but the world and the lore set behind it all makes me want another book in this series. —Nicholas, Amazon.com

Shadows Rising
Scan the QR Code for more!

Book one of the Chronicles of Ash series follows the story of Ash, a 13-year-old boy who was abandoned as a baby. He learns he can control lightning when he has an outburst with his adoptive father. After fleeing, Ash meets other people like him. Together, he and his new friends face a dark enemy that aims to destroy the magic that keeps their island alive, and they must work as a team to stop him.

9 798990 158153